SEX & SATISFACTION

SEX & SATISFACTION

A collection of twenty erotic stories

Edited by Cathryn Cooper

Published by Accent Press Ltd – 2007
ISBN 9781905170777
Reprinted 2008
Reprinted 2009

Printed and bound in the UK by
CPI Bookmarque

Cover Design by
Red Dot Design

Contents

The Blue Roman
by Cathryn Cooper

'Are you going to buy me a drink or what?'

I remember stammering a bit at first. My experience with women was minimal. But I got her a drink anyway. I know now that she was a patsy. I bought her a drink, I had another. Each drink I drank, she got a cut. That was the way things were at the Blue Roman. But I didn't know that then. I was just glad to have someone to talk to about my troubles. Besides, she smelt delicious. Her perfume was like a drug. The more I breathed it in, the more it filled my head. I drank more too. The more I drank, the more I let loose about how crappy it was working at the DA's office. I thought I had the makings of a really good DA, if someone would just give me the chance.

'The DA's office?'

I vaguely recall a certain look coming to her eyes just then, but didn't give it too much account. I was too wrapped up in myself, my personal life and my career prospects to notice anything much.

'Never you mind, honey,' she said, patting my arm. 'I think I know someone who might be able to pull a few strings for you.'

I don't remember quite what I said then. I only remember taking a swig from my glass as she sauntered off to a table half hidden behind some curtains.

Her painted fingernails landed on my arm just as I was ordering another drink. My head was spinning, but, hey, what the hell! I didn't care.

'I want you to meet someone,' she said.

I followed where she led like a dog following a bitch on heat. At least I hoped she was on heat. That was the kind of dog I was.

'Hi there,' said the guy. He was dark and swarthy, Sicilian I suppose. I didn't care. Chloe, as I heard him call her, was nibbling my ear and fondling my ass. I didn't care where he was from as long as the broad kept fondling my crack.

'I hear you're a guy who wants to go places,' he said. There were two other guys with him. I didn't catch their names but took a seat when it was offered.

Chloe's fingers ran down my jacket and onto my thigh. I fixed my attention on the guys though it was far from easy, especially when her hand dived between my legs.

'We can fix anything for you,' said the swarthy-looking guy.

My senses reeled; not due to the generosity of his offer, but because Chloe had disappeared beneath the table and was doing things to my cock.

I felt my buttons being undone, my underwear being adjusted.

'Call me Blue,' said the guy.

I gasped as a pair of plump lips sucked at my dick.

He smiled.

'As I said, I can get you anything. Chloe's proof of that.'

2

So that was it. He knew she was beneath the table licking my mushroom, running her tongue town my stalk. Her teeth nipped at my thatch. I wanted to joke that I didn't need a haircut at present, but on the other hand I understood that this was a serious blow job. Why interrupt a good thing?

He started talking business – about warning him if the Feds were planning to raid his cross-border activities – you know – booze from Canada. I had to force myself to listen. Chloe was cupping my balls, her painted nails pleasantly scratching my scrotum – doing a far better job than when I do it myself, I can tell you.

Anyway, I was having trouble trying to bring my lips together to speak – mostly because the tip of my dick had hit the back of Chloe's throat. Her palms were warm and moist around my stem and her fingers were groping behind my sac and heading for my 'G' spot.

It seemed crazy! Exhilarating! Around us people were dancing and getting drunk, the whole speakeasy skipping and swaying to the throb of a black-faced jazz trio. And I was in a world of my own; my dick was now trapped between Chloe's perfect pair. The tip of my knob was still in her mouth. My love machine was surrounded with flesh – female flesh. I felt I was being devoured by her body; I secretly hoped she'd be up for a second helping!

Blue was carrying on talking as though being sucked to distraction while talking business was the most normal thing in the world.

The guy next to him, who he called Ice, raised a podgy hand. Each finger sported a glittering gold ring. He waved a warning finger. 'Play ball with us, and we'll play ball with you.'

I wanted to say that as long as it was Chloe playing

with my balls that was fine by me.

My dick was jerking as though it wanted to leave my body. Feeling it would be impolite to gasp my orgasm across at Blue and his pals, I held my breath. My body meanwhile shivered with the intensity of it. Like when a long extinct volcano erupts, I shot a hotter, bigger load than on an everyday event. Chloe gulped down every drop. Once she was satisfied she'd swallowed the lot, she wiped my slick tip against her hair before putting my cock away. I guessed she was the sort who liked things to be neat and tidy.

Sensing I was finished, Blue smiled. 'She does a good job, huh?'

I agreed that she did. My cock had been tucked back in my underwear and my flies were re-buttoned.

'So,' said Blue, a fat cigar protruding from the side of his mouth. 'How do you like my place?'

Due to Chloe diverting my attention, I hadn't taken in much of my surroundings until now. She'd made her excuses and gone to powder her nose. I guessed it might be pretty shiny by now from her burrowing among my pubic hairs.

'I know,' said Blue, his black button eyes glinting with amusement. 'You were otherwise engaged.' He waved the cigar at the Romanesque pillars surrounding the central dance floor. 'See those pillars? Some nights I've got nubile young men facing those pillars, their hands chained above their heads, and cute little strips of cloth separating their buttocks. Any member of the audience is entitled to stroke them if they wish. None of the young men will complain of such handling. They're volunteers. Every man jack of 'em!'

I noticed the fat Italian on his left licked his lips.

4

A tall woman with breasts the size of melons came up and whispered in Blue's ear.

'Ah,' he exclaimed, his grin broad enough to divide his face in half. 'We have a cabaret.'

He whispered something back to the woman and nodded approvingly. I wondered what was next, but didn't really care. Nothing could possibly surpass Chloe's performance, could it?

A couch upholstered in red velvet appeared. It had leather belts and other things hanging from it, facts that became obvious as it was upended, the foot of the bed fastened to the floor.

The jazz musicians blew a fanfare on their brass. Four dancers marched onto the stage wearing leather corsets that were no more than a strip between their legs, a belt around their waists and straps that kind of scooped beneath their breasts and over their shoulders. They also wore high boots that came half way up their thighs and were attached by suspenders to their belts. On their heads they wore Roman-style helmets with leather visors that came down over their eyes. Each of them carried a whip, and as they danced they cracked them in time to the band.

All conversation ceased. A strange apprehension glowed in people's eyes when suddenly the music stopped. One of the dancers stepped forward.

'I demand justice! Someone here has been messing around where she shouldn't have been messing.'

Standing like a gladiator, she looked straight at Blue.

'That's for the audience to decide,' he said. 'Ask them.'

A thrill of electricity ran through those watching.

The chief dancer spoke again. 'I say this adulteress should be stripped naked and punished by other women. What say you?'

Put like that – the mention of nakedness – the whole audience went wild.

A gasp went up when two of the dancers leapt forward and dragged a woman out of the audience.

I licked the dryness from my mouth and barely stopped myself from leaping onto the table to get an even better view than I already had. But that, I decided, would be ill-mannered.

The woman had red hair tightly fastened in an old fashioned bun. It came adrift and floated around her shoulders when she struggled. She looked terrified, crying out that it wasn't her.

I had no doubt it was all a put-up job; she was one of the cast and knew exactly what was about to happen. It didn't matter. My cock was leaping in my pants. I guess everyone else's was too. Even the women must have been seeping with excitement.

The girls asked the guy she'd been sitting with if their accusation was true and that he belonged to someone else.

Well, he wasn't going to spoil the fun was he? Like everybody else, his eyes were on stalks.

The girls stripped the girl and fastened her face down to the upended couch. They asked the audience how many strokes of the whip she should have. I think they decided one from each girl – for starters.

The first stroke landed. The girl screamed. The lead dancer decided they couldn't have that sort of noise in a respectable establishment, and had one of her minions gag her.

Her bottom was quite red after half a dozen strokes. They began to unfasten the leather wrist and ankle cuffs that held her there. I thought that was the end of it, but I was wrong. They turned her round.

Her breasts jiggled provocatively; her stomach was as flat as a pancake which served to accentuate her fiery red nest. Her waist was narrow and her hips flaring in the kind of curves you want to lick with your tongue.

I could almost hear the audience salivating, and I didn't need much imagination to know that there were more than a few stiff pricks and wet crotches in the audience.

'This is what you like, isn't it?' one of the leather-clad girls said to the one tied up. She squeezed the girl's breast and played around with her nipple. Another girl did the same to the other breast. The other two pulled the outer lips of her sex aside; those at the front of the audience leaned forward to get a better view of the slick, velvety interior.

There was no way the girl could not respond to that sort of treatment; they were pressing all the right buttons. Within no time, the girl's hips were jerking against their fingertips. Everyone could see her sex getting glossier and twitchier. Her hips jerked and the dirty bitch even had the nerve to open her legs even wider. Each girl took it in turn to sink her fingers into the bound girl's juicy fruit, finger-fucking her for all they were worth. With their free hands they rolled her tits about, pushing them together so the nipples almost kissed, sucking them until they were long enough to use as coat hooks.

At last her whole body shook with climax, her eyes rolled in her head before closing, and like the tide, her body surged with release before ebbing away into calm repose.

The audience burst into applause.

I thought that was the end of it, but I was wrong.

Someone shouted for an encore.

I saw the dancers exchange knowing smiles. There was

more. My dick jerked in my pants. I looked around for Chloe and her delicious mouth. I had need of her services.

The lead dancer, the same one as before, stood centre stage, knuckles resting on hips, a faint sheen of sweat glistening on her naked breasts. She held her head high and looked to be enjoying herself.

'This broad likes more than one fuck per week and with more than one man. She might as well have a few more. You're all invited to have a go. Now,' she said, as murmurs of wild excitement swept through the audience.

'I'll go first.'

I couldn't believe I'd said it, but there I was making my way forward.

The lead dancer smiled, glanced down at the front of my pants, saw that I was up for it, and looked directly into my face.

'So. How do you want her?'

I didn't fancy the thought of entering her as she was, my ass facing the audience. After all, they were paying to see her ass not mine.

'Down on all fours.'

The legs of the bed were brought back to the floor. The girls got the redhead into position, the leather straps readjusted.

I unbuttoned my flies, hoping that the stiffness in my dick wasn't down to imagination. I glanced down. So did the girls, expressions of admiration brightening their faces.

Obligingly, the girls held the girl's buttocks apart so I could more easily penetrate. I slid into her void like a steel rod into a velvet glove. She gripped me tight. I pounded and pounded, slamming my pubic bone against her ass, my balls swinging and slapping her clit.

As I slammed, the two girls holding her buttocks apart kissed me and fondled my ass. One of the others fondled the redhead's breast, while the other fingered her clitoris and tickled my balls each time they came within reach.

I kept going, wanting to spurt but unwilling to come too soon and stand aside for the next guy. I wanted to be the first – and the best!

'Now her ass,' shouted the lead dancer, taking me completely unawares.

Now usually a little lubricant is called for – a little saliva, some kind of gel; this girl came armed with champagne.

Slick with the redhead's juices, my dick slid out but stood firmly to attention when I caught sight of the champagne being poured between her buttocks. My cock head lapped it up.

The girls held her cheeks away from her tight little rosebud. At first I tickled it, teased it a little, then inch by slowly disappearing inch, I pushed it in.

She arched her back, her smooth behind brushing my loins as I hit target, buried up to the hilt.

Someone was kissing my balls. I don't know who and didn't care. For the second time that night I gushed hot lava into a willing vent.

Blue collared me before I left. 'You'll have to come again. You know you Feds are always welcome here.' He stuffed a fifty into my top pocket. 'That's for services rendered – now and in the future.'

I checked my hat and looked back only briefly before leaving. A queue had formed behind the willing redhead. Her gag was off and besides being plugged at the back she was sucking on a dick, her hands clutching his scary white shanks.

I smiled to myself as the big bruiser on the door let me out.

'See you again,' he said as though it were a foregone conclusion.

'I doubt it,' I muttered once the door was safely closed behind me. Yes, I had been a federal agent, but that was all behind me now. Like I was trying to tell Chloe when I'd first gone in, I'd got the chop and all because my rampant wife ran out on me and I'd fallen apart. But I'd heard rumours and had wanted to see her again. She'd always wanted to be on the stage, and now she'd achieved it. I'd just wanted to fuck her one more time. And I had. Now she was anybody's; literally.

Netsuke
by N. Vasco

'Tell if you like,' Jim heard as he walked into the Oriental gift shop.

The store was empty except for an old Asian woman sitting behind the counter, her dark, slanted eyes giving him a curious look as he walked down a narrow aisle lined with shelves displaying all kinds of curios and gifts.

He sniffed the air and noticed a smoking incense stick sticking out of a small jade box on the counter where the lady sat.

'Smells nice in here,' he said, trying to strike up a conversation.

She didn't respond. She watched him explore the shelves until he walked up to the counter and said, 'I'm looking for a gift…for a woman.'

She responded with a sly smile, before stepping from behind the counter and leading him to the back room. That's when he noticed the graceful, leaf-shaped gold armlet on her right arm and the tight mandarin dress she wore. His gaze travelled down to her nicely shaped backside, her trim yet curvy hips swaying with each step, a hint of ivory thigh peering from the waist high slits, as the 'tap' of her black, stiletto heels echoed in the dim interior.

A little too provocative for someone's grandmother, Jim thought. But a nice ass.

The old woman must have read his mind. She looked at him and giggled as they stopped in front of a wall lined with shelves. Jim avoided her gaze but was unprepared for the spectacle before him.

They stood in front of a table covered with phalluses of every size, colour and texture. On the shelves were dozens of three-inch high, nude figurines. He gazed at a riot of naked men and women. Some masturbated by themselves. Others were involved in everything from one on one sex to orgies that would've broken the laws in a few states.

She selected a woman kneeling with her mouth wide open and said, 'Called *netsuke*. Very detailed, yes?' She turned it to reveal tiny painted hairs around two holes. One for the pussy. Another for the anus.

'Very realistic. Arrange anyway you like,' the woman said. She placed a kneeling man with an erection behind the woman and slid the porcelain cock into the anus.

'I guess,' Jim replied. His gaze wandered to the figurine of a dark-haired beauty lying on a jade couch. He saw a tiny gold band around the arm.

The old woman noticed this and picked it up. 'You like?'

Embarrassed, Jim backed away.

'No…that's okay,' he said and bumped against the table, almost knocking down a big phallus. He picked it up without thinking, waved it around and said, 'I was just looking for a vase or…jewellery box.'

Noticing what it was he was waving around, he set it down quickly and blushed.

The woman seemed disappointed. She pointed to the

front.

'Vases near window. Go pick one. I give good price.'

Jim hurried to front of the store. He quickly scanned the shelves, found a very proper looking vase and walked back to the counter where the old woman was wrapping a small parcel. She smiled, rang up the vase, gave him the change and handed over the parcel.

'I didn't pay for that'' Jim said.

'A gift. You like incense, yes?' she said while pressing the package in his hand.

He stammered. 'Yes, but…'

The woman stepped from behind the counter, led him to the door and said, 'You take…a gift!' She opened the door, the sound of the chimes almost drowned out by the passing traffic. Jim found himself pushed outside.

'I have to close…you open tonight before sleep. Enjoy!'

Bright sunlight and loud traffic greeted his eyes and ears. The woman locked the door and pulled down the shade. His beeper went off. It was the office.

Damn! he thought, I'll be late for the afternoon meeting. He shuffled the packages in his hands, 'I'll come back to tomorrow and return this thing,' he said to himself and walked back to the office.

Natalie, Jim's secretary, admired the vase's intricate designs. 'I love it, where did you get it?'

'The Oriental shop down the street,' Jim responded.

She gave him a confused look. 'I thought that place was closed for the week. I know the owner. He's on vacation with his niece.'

'It was open. An older Asian woman was at the counter.'

13

'Well, it's mine now.' She smiled and flounced off to show it to the other secretaries.

Jim got home tired and puzzled. The shop had been closed, so Natalie said. But it hadn't. It was open.

After a quick shower he put on his pyjamas, sat on his bed and opened the old woman's gift.

'Might as well see what it's like,' he muttered while unwrapping it.

It was a jade incense box adorned with designs and fine patterns he couldn't make out. A few incense sticks and a small object wrapped in red paper lay inside. After unwrapping it he saw to his surprise it was the nude Asian woman on the jade couch.

'Great! Now I have to go back tomorrow. She'll probably say I stole it.'

He stared at the figurine. It was real, so detailed. Her body was perfectly proportioned, the nipples dark and full, tipping a pair of round, inviting breasts. The hips tapered from a small waist and led to a pair of smooth, shapely legs. The eyes were half-closed, the full, red lips tempting and seductive.

'I wonder what it would be like to kiss those lips,' Jim thought, feeling his cock stir.

He sighed, ran his fingers along the tiny, yet perfect body and thought how pathetic he was. Here I am getting horny over a porcelain figure.

Lighting an incense stick he placed it through one of the holes on the box. On lying down he saw the bulge of his cock under the sheets and said out loud, 'Guess you won't let me sleep tonight.' He wrapped his hand around the stiff member but decided he didn't feel like masturbating. The incense had a calming effect. After a

14

deep breath Jim felt himself sliding into sleep, still feeling the hardness of his erection in his fist.

After what seemed like a few seconds, he woke up naked under the sheets and immediately turned to look at the incense stick. It was still burning but the figurine was missing. Hearing a noise, he turned and saw the most beautiful sight in his entire life.

A gorgeous Asian woman with long black hair and wearing a tight red mandarin dress stood next to his bed. Creamy thighs and hips peeked out of waist high slits and the outline of her nipples pressed against the thin fabric. She bowed politely and sat next to him. She smelled of cherry blossom.

As she leaned close to his face, Jim recognized the leaf-shaped band on her right arm. Before he could make any comment, she held the back of his head and gave him a deep, passionate kiss. Her breath tasted sweeter than honey and she purred like a kitten as her tongue gently probed into his mouth.

Might as well enjoy this dream, he thought as he leaned into her kiss. Raising his hands, he gently massaged her supple back.

The purr turned into a moan. She responded by kneading his arms and chest. It was his turn to gasp when her long red nails glided over the area just above his throbbing cock.

This has got to be the fullest, hardest ass I've ever held, he thought squeezing her firm yet pliant buttocks.

She leaned back, gave him a playful smile and pulled down the sheets, exposing his penis. Her eyes glistened like two black pools. She crossed her legs, allowing her thighs and most of her hips to emerge from the slits of her dress.

'Am I glad I'm a leg man,' Jim said.

She gave him a coy look, took his hand and ran it over her bare thighs, stomach and the inviting swell of her right breast. Her nipples seemed to dig into his palm. Then she climbed on the bed, straddled his chest and undid her dress in a slow, languid manner. The red fabric cascaded down her body revealing the creamy glory of her upturned, generously tipped breasts, her slim waist and inviting hips.

Jim instantly feasted on her nipples, making her gasp and hiss as his hand travelled to the wet, silky hairs of her crotch. His finger slipped into the tightest pussy he had ever encountered. Her gasping turned into deep, throaty moans.

She sat up, took his fingers from her crotch and licked the juices with her darting tongue.

Jim understood. He eased down to her thighs, his tongue travelling over her moist, puffy lips and into her juicy love hole. He sucked at her prissy little clit, nibbling and blowing his breath over the hard little bud. She giggled with delight. He glanced up, saw her enjoying her breasts and resumed his feast, alternating between deep probes and gentle nibbles.

The technique worked. He felt her buttocks clench and writhe. She arched her back, gave a loud moan that was almost a scream and uttered her only word for the night.

'Yes!'

Her body seemed to collapse for a moment. She got off his face, cuddled on the pillow next to his and lapped her juices off his cheeks, lips and chin. Her tongue licked his neck as she pressed his veined meat between her breasts and rubbed his throbbing pole, making him gasp as a faint stream of jism shot out and land on her right cheek.

16

Must be ready to come, he thought, shrugging an apology.

She just smiled, wiped her cheek and licked the pearly drop off her palm. Her face now hovered just above his hard member. She licked the tip, playfully bit the head and ran her tongue over his shaft before parting her lips and drawing him into her mouth.

Feels like butterfly wings, he thought as her lips enveloped him. She sucked gently at first, then harder, moving her exquisite face up and down as she reached up with one hand and began to toy with his nipples. His pulse surged in his ears as he gripped the sheets and gasped for air. Her other hand reached between his legs gently scratching his tense sac.

The surge in his body became a torrent of pleasure he could barely control until that familiar, hot, wet feeling gushed out of his body and exploded in her mouth. He could barely hear her loud, sucking sounds, her almost purr-like moans making that whisky mouth gently vibrate, sending ripples of pleasure until…

Jim woke up.

He was alone, in his bed, still in his pyjamas. He looked under the sheets, expecting a wet, sticky coating on his pants.

He was dry.

'Strangest wet dream I ever had,' he murmured.

He looked at the night table. The figurine was there, next to the incense box, the wick now small and spent.

The last thing Jim thought of was the face on the figurine. He eyed her closely and was surprised to see her expression seemed changed. She looked pleased, and dare he think it, satisfied.

He stopped by the store the next day and rattled the door handle. No one at home. The only thing greeting him was a 'closed' sign indicating the owners would return in a week.

That night, his cock stirring at the memory of the previous night, he decided to light the incense one more time.

It was just a dream, he thought. Something in his mind said otherwise as the aroma covered him and he drifted into sleep. The last thing he saw before his eyes closed was the figurine, her skin seeming to shine with life.

He woke up on a mat in a room lined with black and red panels, glossy in the glow of Chinese lanterns. He was naked underneath a black cotton kimono.

One of the panels slid aside as he got up. Two lovely oriental girls in tight Chinese dresses stepped into the room. One wore red, the other green.

Although the air was warm their nipples pressed against the silky fabric, the ivory glory of their naked hips and thighs peering from the waist-high slits.

Smiling seductively, the girls bowed and introduced themselves.

The girl in the green dress bowed first. 'I'm Jade.'

Eyes twinkling, the other girl followed. 'I'm Pearl.'

Jim made the decision to follow their example and got to his feet. Bowing proved quite astonishing, the motion making his erection poke out from his kimono.

Jade and Pearl giggled.

Blushing, he covered his exposed member and tried to regain some semblance of control. It didn't work.

Seeing his embarrassment, the girls exchanged knowing glances and guided him to a corridor illuminated by paper lamps, finally stepping through an open panel into another room.

Paper lanterns hanging from ornate dragons' heads set into the walls cast a warm, yellow light on the floor mats.

Taking his hands in theirs, the girls led him to a chair. He sat down full of excitement, his knob piercing through the opening in his kimono like some kind of oriental obelisk.

Pearl began undressing, her silky attire falling to the ground and revealing a luscious, naked body.

He didn't know why he hadn't felt Jade tying his hands to the chair, and although he struggled, he didn't really mind that much, especially when Jade diverted his attention. The green silk dress slid off her body; she stood naked and inviting, her flesh almost golden in the glow of lantern light.

Both girls turned their backs to each other and bent over, slowly rubbing each other's round buttocks, their pleasing sighs and purring moans music to his ears. Then, Jade turned and ran her nipples down Pearl's back before kneeling, her pliant fingers probing the wet, luscious crotch in front of her face.

Jim was very aware that his cock had acquired a mind of its own; even if his hands had been free, nothing would have stopped it standing proud. Oh, how it ached for their attention, for just one of them to finger its sweating tip or lick its length with their delicate tongues.

The girls continued to perform in front of him, Jade now enjoying the oral ministrations of Pearl's invading tongue.

Jim groaned. This was torture. Pure hell in fact! Two gorgeous Asian beauties pleasing each other's naked bodies and all he could do was watch.

19

A gong suddenly sounded. A panel slid open. Jade and Pearl ceased their activities, stood and bowed as a figure in a black robe, the face hidden behind a golden mask, glided into the room.

Unsure who the new person was and what might happen next, Jim's erection went soft. Would his dream turn into a nightmare?

Both girls crawled on all fours to the robed person, but not even the sight of their pretty asses could allay his concern.

On reaching the figure, each girl was raised to her feet by a pair of beautiful hands emerging from the dark fabric. Long red nails and noble fingers adorned by gold rings glistened in the candlelight.

Still tense in his body and flaccid in his cock, Jim watched his fear dissipating once he glimpsed the glitter of a gold band on the left arm.

Jade pulled down the hood as Pearl undid the robe. The mask was removed.

It was her! The woman from his dream!

She smiled at him as the robe slid off her body, revealing the same creamy skin and ample curves from the night before.

Pearl and Jade took the lids off tall jars standing to either side of her, dipped their hands in and brought them out again. The scent of mimosa and jasmine filled the air as they rubbed the scented oil all over the woman's body.

What a show, Jim thought as two pairs of delicate hands massaged oil over the woman's ivory breasts, stomach and inviting hips.

The woman smiled directly at him as Pearl knelt and began licking her pussy. Jim groaned. He could still remember the way it tasted, sweet with just a hint of tartness. Jade wasted no time. She ran her tongue down her mistress's back, over the cleft of her perfect ass and began licking her anus.

The woman was gasping in delight as both girls probed her luscious flower and delectable backdoor. She gave Jim a wicked, inviting look and tapped Jade's shoulder. The girl giggled, got up and ran to him. Kneeling, she untied the ropes, took him by the hand and led him to her mistress, her lowered eyes admiring his throbbing meat.

By now Pearl and the woman were on the floor, their heads buried between each other's luscious thighs. Quickly, and without any sign of her intention, Pearl rolled underneath, grabbed her mistress's buttocks and revealed the inviting site of her anus. Jade knelt, pulled Jim down onto his knees, took his cock in her dainty hands and guided him until he was just out outside of the rim of the woman's tight rosebud.

Jade pressed his back, allowing him to slowly glide inside.

Jim gasped with delight. He had never experienced anal sex before. The sensation was like having a tight velvet glove surrounding his shaft.

Inching slowly inwards, he relished the sensation of her body slowly yielding to his penetration. He pumped gently, determined that she would enjoy the exercise as much as he was. He didn't care if it was a dream or not. He didn't want to force or hurt her. The woman sensed this. The sight of her exotic, catlike eyes looking at him over her shoulder was almost enough to make him come, but not yet. Sensing his concern for her, she said her first word for the night.

'Deeper.'

Jim obliged. He slid further into her back door; she

moaned and hissed more loudly. Her body shuddered under his and her rounded cheeks pressed against his lap.

As he continued to thrust, Pearl feasted on her mistress's breasts while Jade massaged the woman's clitoris with her delicate fingers, sometimes licking Jim's nipples, sometimes kissing the woman's red lips.

Gradually, that delicious, warm feeling coursing through his body accumulated into a gush of pleasure that ached for release. The sensation spread so quickly and so intensely until he felt ready to shatter into a million pieces. Just when he felt he couldn't wait any longer, she peered at him over her ivory shoulders and gasped the word he wanted to hear.

'Yes!!'

His body racked and heaved. Her hands reached round and clutched his buttocks pressing him in even deeper. And then it happened. Suddenly his pleasure gushed out of his body. Pearl and Jade continued their tongue-probing kisses and erotic caresses until...

He woke up.

Still in his pyjamas.

In his bed.

Alone.

He looked for the figurine. It was gone.

He almost tore his apartment apart that night, looking for the naked oriental beauty of his dreams. Frustrated, he went to sleep, alone and tired.

A week later, acting purely on instinct, he went to the store. The chimes rang as he entered. An old man sat behind the counter and asked, 'Can I help you?'

Jim didn't know what to say. He'd expected the old woman.

'Yes...where is the lady that was here three days ago?'

22

The man gave a quizzical look. 'We've been closed. I was on vacation with my niece.'

Feeling a bit of a fool, Jim avoided the old man's questioning look. He pretended to be interested in looking around the shop. Suddenly his gaze fell on a black and white photo of a woman under the glass counter. He stared and when he saw the old man's hands grab the picture began to mutter an apology.

'Sorry. I didn't mean to be rude…'

The old man smiled and set the picture on the counter.

Jim tensed. The picture was old but the woman sitting on the ornate chair looked familiar. She wore a tight fitting, mandarin dress with a waist high slit on either side. A gold, leaf-shaped band encircled her left arm.

'That's my wife,' the old man said.

Jim looked up, startled. He didn't know if he should feel scared or guilty.

'Your wife?'

'Yes, she died two years ago. She made me the happiest man alive.' The old man eyed the picture fondly. 'She promised me her soul would not rest until she found the perfect man for our daughter.'

The door chimes rang. A feminine voice called 'Father! I brought lunch!'

Jim turned as a beautiful Asian woman in business attire walked up to the counter.

'Xia!' the old man said. 'We were talking about your mother.'

The girl turned to Jim and smiled. 'Hello.'

The clear bell of her voice rang in his ear. His eyes travelled over a tight yet lusciously curved body her tailored business suit seemed to cling to. A mane of black, lustrous hair surrounded her delicate face.

Her coal black eyes smiled back at him, her eyebrows a pair of startled raven's wings, her coral lips slightly parted, revealing pearly teeth.

His throat felt very tight, the 'Hello' he finally managed to give her sounding more like a croak through the surging pulse in his ear.

The old man noticed how they stared at each other. He glanced at his wife's picture then turned back to Jim.

'Won't you join us for lunch?'

Jim couldn't hide his surprise. 'I wouldn't want to intrude.'

For some reason this made the old man laugh. 'I'll set another place!'

He left the two of them alone.

Jim looked at the bag Xia held.

'Let me help you.'

'Thank you,' she replied.

He stood with the bag in his hand and watched as she removed her blazer, revealing a gossamer sleeveless blouse.

Suddenly, Jim's mind reeled. It wasn't the way her blouse clung to her high, upturned breasts and the way the silken fabric hinted at the sublime yet generous outline of her erect nipples. It was the gold, leaf shaped band she wore on her left arm and the way it seemed to glisten with a light of its own.

She noticed him staring.

'It used to belong to my mother. Some people think it's too provocative.'

She stepped a little closer, a coy, playful look on her delicate face and gave him a delightfully questioning smile, the inviting contours of her body now inches away.

'What do you think?'

He smiled while gazing into those two dark pools.
'I like it very much.'

Any Day of the Week
by Jeremy Edwards

'You're obsessed with my ass, aren't you?' said Nadine, as she scooted the aforementioned attribute onto the passenger seat of my car.

'What do you mean?' I asked this question knowing, of course, exactly what she meant.

She gave me a perfunctory, after-work kiss. 'I mean that you look at it the way most people look at a sunset.'

'I can take or leave sunsets,' I explained. Her ass, tonight, was wearing the lime capris within which it looked more mesmerizing than a hundred sunsets: in my humble opinion.

'I can take or leave my ass,' she shrugged. 'I don't see what's so special about it. Even when I stand totally nude in front of a three-way mirror, all I see are six boring buttocks.'

A punctual erection challenged my ready-to-drive-the-car posture. As I answered Nadine's observation, I grasped the parking brake – classic displacement, if you're of the Viennese school.

'That's why it's my job, and not yours, to appreciate this ass we speak of. Furthermore, I defy you to find anything in our vehicle more deserving of my obsessive fascinations.'

She smiled. 'Always the logical one, aren't you. I guess I'm just blasé.'

I patted her hand and attempted to put things in perspective. 'You're not blasé. You're just *ass* blasé. And not even consistently. For example, you weren't blasé about your ass last Saturday night, when I was squeezing and tickling and patting and fondling it...and, if I recall correctly, you emphatically urged me to keep doing all of the above.' I recalled correctly, all right.

'Did I? I don't remember.'

'It certainly looked like you, anyway.' I put the car in gear.

'Fine. So I'm *un*-ass-blasé on weekends. I'll collect my prize at the door. But this is Monday, and we need to get groceries more than we need to talk about my ass.'

'Speak for yourself. But I concede that we do need some groceries.' I always try to meet her halfway in these situations.

We pulled out of the parking lot of Nadine's workplace. I had picked her up here almost every weeknight for years, and I'd learned that the post-work decompress was not the time to catch her in a sexy frame of mind. She was tired, preoccupied...and unnervingly practical. She was hot stuff from 5:00 Friday till midnight on Sunday; but it was as if all her sexual mechanisms shut down during the work week – as if the hormones went into hibernation and the libido went out of town on business.

As we drove the two miles to the supermarket that evening, I realized that I wanted desperately to seduce Nadine on a weeknight. We'd been together for three years, sleeping in the same bed every night and rocking

28

each other's socks on weekends. Now I was intent on coaxing the socks-rocking side of her personality out of its dormancy on a Monday night. Everyone needs a hobby.

In the weeks that followed, we observed our accustomed rhythm – hectic activity and quasi-platonic companionship during the week, capped by abandoned sexual indulgence on weekends. I relished the weekends as much as ever, but my desire to carry our lust across the weekday threshold was becoming increasingly strong by lingering unfulfilled. Nor had I neglected the task of trying to fulfil it. Every Monday, I hinted, I caressed, I teased…but her response always extended to affectionate appreciation, and no further.

Spring turned to summer. When we got home with the groceries one Monday night in late June, we were both drenched with what the meteorologists quaintly call relative humidity. I made a gambit.

'Whew! I don't know about you, but I'm ready to put on some fresh clothes,' I prompted. Nadine concurred.

'Since you have to change anyway, how about wearing the blue skirt?' Though I tried to sound casual, the significance of this suggestion was clear to us both. She owned several blue skirts, and she knew precisely which one I meant. My favourite. The mini. Iridescent peacock blue. Always, by household custom, worn without panties.

She spoke tenderly but decisively. 'Bernard, I've absolutely got to work on that presentation this evening. I'll be up and down from computer to printer to fax for the next three or four hours. Do you really want to see my cunt every time I sit, stand up, and bend down?'

Hmph. She wouldn't have asked a question like that on a Friday. 'Of course I do.'

She shrugged.

'You know,' I teased, 'you're not only ass-blasé, I think you're also c –'

'Shh! I'm getting the skirt, okay? We sincerely hope you'll enjoy yourself...but don't take it as a commitment on my part.' Her eyes twinkled – playfully but not, I had to admit, lasciviously. Not yet. She smiled indulgently at me before bopping briskly into the walk-in closet.

I got myself a microbrew and a Wodehouse, made myself comfortable on the loveseat that faced her workstation, and settled in for a challenging evening. Was I correct in surmising that she could not go sans panties all evening without becoming aroused?

Nadine had been at the computer for about forty-five minutes when, out of the corner of my eye, I saw her hand dart between her thighs and her hips subtly pivot.

I'm the kind of person who is not above saying 'Aha!' This I now did.

'Aha! It may be Monday...but you, my dear, are getting horny.'

What I'd phrased as a fact was really just optimistic speculation, and I cocked a hopeful eyebrow her way as I awaited confirmation.

She gave me a weary but tolerant look. 'I have to pee, if you must know.'

'Indeed, I must.' I am nothing if not adaptable, and I was right behind her as she headed toward the powder room. 'Mind if I come with?' Nadine has pointed out that I have a tendency to drop objective pronouns when aroused.

She paused outside the door, turned, and shook her head dismissively. 'I'm right in the middle of what I'm doing. I was hoping to make it quick in there.'

It was hard to believe that this was the same woman who – only a couple of Saturdays ago – had phoned me

30

from a toilet seat in Nordstrom's ladies' room to tell me she was having the best piss of her life, and that she wanted me to listen. 'Wish you were here,' she'd giggled, like a kinky postcard. Now I *was* here, but business was just business. I waited just outside the bathroom door as the brief auditory parade of waterfall, paper-tearing and flush marked her efficient absence with musical precision. Her efficiency made me all the more aroused.

She settled back into her work, and I bided my time. Apart from studiously including her in my field of vision, I did not intrude on Nadine's agenda while she worked at the computer, dashed to the printer, and ferried documents to the fax machine. But every time she rose, sat, or even shifted positions, I got a glimpse of cunt. And I began to notice that her eyes usually met mine, just instantaneously, after such a moment. It was as if she were silently asking, 'Did you see my cunt that time? Did you see it?' It was driving me wild to know that she knew, all the time she was working, that she had an exposed cunt, and that I was watching, waiting for it to wink at me. And that, somewhere beneath her conscientious attention to her all-absorbing business presentation, she was, I could sense, turned on by this.

I began to hone in on her rhythm. Her fingers tapping on the keyboard, her legs shifting position, her papers rustling…these themes interacted to establish an erotic beat that was punctuated by her unconscious flashing, which was becoming more frequent. Tappity-tap WINK rustle-rustle WINK shift-rustle-rustle-shift WINK.

And, every time she flashed me, I looked for the first hint of wetness. At last, at the moment when she momentarily parted and closed her legs in conjunction with a particularly emphatic click of the mouse, I was sure

31

I saw lips that subtly glistened. I put down my book and gave her my full attention, waiting for the next development.

When I seemed to see her hand flit once again between her legs a few minutes later, the motion was so quick that I wasn't sure of what I'd seen, despite my unwavering focus.

'Horny now?' I asked, in a tone falsely calm, as though my interest were mere idle curiosity.

'Um, I –' She was actually blushing. My pulse began to race.

'I thought I saw you touching yourself.'

'I don't remember. I was concentrating.' She tried to get back to work.

I stood and walked toward her, meeting her eyes and offering what I hoped was my most seductive smile. 'Concentrating or not, you can at least tell if you're getting wet, can't you?'

'Fuck!' she suddenly said.

'I thought you'd never ask.'

'It wasn't a request, Bernard, it was a garden-variety expletive. I just lost a contact lens.'

'Oh. Well then, let me help you find it.' I began to explore the carpet at her feet. I didn't see the lens. I looked up, about to relay the bad news. But, as I raised my eyes, I found it. It had dropped onto the edge of her skirt. And, just as I spied it, it toppled a bit further and came delicately to rest on her person, nesting exquisitely in her bush. I grinned from ear to ear.

'Don't move.'

'I won't. Where is it?'

'Where indeed. Hold perfectly still.' I kissed her ankle.

'Mmm,' she said involuntarily, and her legs twitched.

32

'What are you doing?'

'Kissing your ankle,' I specified.

'I thought you were picking up my contact lens.'

'I'm multi-tasking.'

'Perhaps you should do a little less multi and a little more tasking,' she suggested. 'Ohh…that feels good,' she added.

I kissed my way up her right leg, as far as the inside of her knee. I paused there to note the effect of my attentions on what a meteorologist might call the 'glisten index' above. I was gratified by what I saw. I began anew on the left leg, beginning once again at the ankle.

'Bernard…'

'I'm busy.'

'No, *I'm* busy. You're distracting me. Ohhh, wow…' I had just reached the back of her left knee, where I lingered. Her legs were definitely indulging in a hip-driven swivel now, and her cunt was morphing from a pair of tight, glistening lips into a moist, yawning creature that wakes up hungry.

The contact lens was still resting safely in her thatch, so I knew I could stretch this out a little longer. I kissed upward along the inside of her left thigh.

'Bernard…oh…the *lens,* Bernard.'

'Got it,' I said. And I had. It was between the thumb and forefinger of my right hand. The other fingers were now pressing gently on Nadine's mound.

I offered up the contact lens, which she claimed, and I immediately returned my hand to the place where I'd found the lens. You never know, I thought – there might be another lens, or something else of importance, lost in her garden. I duly explored the area with gentle motions of my hand. She began to purr, so I inserted the forefinger of

33

my left hand just within her moistening lips. She parted her thighs a bit further and shivered sensuously. I intensified my intimate caress and resumed kissing the most delicate parts of her leg.

Her groan told me that she had psychologically passed the point of no return, had finally resigned herself to a toe-tingling sexual release on this busy Monday night. As I sped up the motion of the finger that tickled her insides, I cooed my admiration.

'You're gorgeous,' I told her. 'Gorgeous,' I repeated. 'GORGEOUS,' I said an unnecessary third time, at a slightly higher volume. By now she was dripping, and I knew that she would want my articulate tongue. I eased my finger out, gently clenched her knee joints, and began to smother her delicate core with wet tastes along every bit of her exposed femininity and within its invisible depths. Every squirm of her ass pressed her hot spots sensuously against the earnest mouth that titillated and sizzled.

As she ground her pussy compulsively against me, her groans intensified and shaped themselves into a consonant. 'Mmm, mmm, mmm,' she intoned, with rhythmic insistence.

My tongue worked harder, and her thighs began to tremble around my ears. Her ass cheeks were hot as fresh-baked rolls. 'Mmm...mmm...' She was trying to say more. As she gasped between the incipient cries of urgent, orgasmic bliss, a word emerged, belted with ecstatic surprise:

'Mmmm...m–m–Mmmonday,' she crooned, shaking, her song diffusing into tender, rapturous whimpers, her cunt kissing me wetly, her arms flopping weakly, gracefully onto my shoulders.

I stood up, and she led me to the loveseat, where she

collapsed on her flank. I had managed to remove only one trouser leg before she reached into my shorts and pulled me toward, on to, and into her. She was so slick that I slid in effortlessly. She was still wearing the peacock blue skirt, and it tickled my belly as I rocked languidly through the few, short moments it took for me to spasm giddily into her slippery, tingling embrace and fill her with sticky weeknight distraction.

Rock Hard
by Kristina Wright

The stadium was packed with thousands of screaming fans as rock star Damien belted out a song with lyrics that seemed meant only for me. I squeezed my husband Eric's hand a little tighter as Damien sang, feeling fuzzy from drinking at the pub before the concert and the one hit I'd take from the joint someone smuggled in. I was so caught up in the sexy voice that I didn't realize that my friend Lydia was waving something at me.

I leaned closer and yelled over the music, 'What's that?'

'How would you like to meet Damien in person?'

'What?'

'Backstage passes,' she said. That's what she was waving. 'Jeff doesn't really care about meeting the band, but I thought you might.'

I nodded enthusiastically. Just the thought of meeting Damien made my heart race.

Eric leaned in from the other side. 'Is that what I think it is?'

I nodded. 'Lydia has backstage passes!'

Eric pressed his lips to my ear and whispered, 'Isn't

Damien on your list of celebrities you'd like to fuck?'

I smacked his arm, even though he was right. We each had a list of celebrities we wanted to have sex with and, of course, Damien was on my list. It was one of those things that couples joke about and never really happens. Still, the alcohol and pot in my system, combined with Damien's incredible voice and Eric's hand on my ass had me fantasizing about the possibilities.

Lydia's husband Jeff noticed where Eric's hand was and winked at me. Eric and I have speculated that Lydia and Jeff might be swingers, though Lydia has never mentioned it. It didn't really matter to me since I couldn't imagine having sex with someone other than Eric and I'm not interested in women. I smiled at Jeff and Lydia, feeling excited and anxious about what the rest of the night held in store.

While the band was doing an encore, Lydia grabbed my hand. 'Let's go before everyone starts leaving.'

Eric gave my ass another squeeze and said, 'Have fun!'

I wasn't sure what he meant, but I nodded. 'See you back at the hotel.'

Lydia gave Jeff a quick kiss and a knowing smile before tugging me toward the backstage entrance.

The next couple of hours were a blur. One minute we were showing our backstage passes to two burly bodyguards, the next we were backstage with the band, and roadies. We couldn't get anywhere near Damien at first because of the crowd of people around him, but we talked with the rest of the band and had a few drinks. I watched Damien from a distance and decided he was just as incredible in person as I had imagined. He was a little rough and wild around the edges, but with a bad boy's charm that made me giggle like a teenager every time he looked in my direction.

Finally, the crowd cleared a bit and Lydia wasted no time in getting close to Damien I was almost jealous when I saw her hand on his arm, running her fingers along his tattoo as she introduced herself. She smiled and held her other hand out to me. 'Come here, Carly. Damien doesn't bite.'

Damien gave me a long, slow look that made my toes curl. 'Unless you want me to.'

'I'll let you do anything you like,' I said.

I couldn't believe the words came out of my mouth until I saw Lydia's eyes widen. I laughed. I didn't know what had come over me, but I blamed the alcohol and excitement of finally meeting Damien in person.

'Where are you girls staying?'

Lydia told him the name of our hotel and he grinned. 'Me, too. Let me give you a ride.'

It was like a dream, riding in a limousine with Damien on the way back to our hotel. Lydia and I sat on either side of him and he had an arm around each of us. It should have felt weird since he was a stranger, but I felt like I knew him. He put his hand on my thigh and, instead of pushing him away, I snuggled closer.

I expected him to disappear with his bodyguards and bandmates when we got back to the hotel. Instead, he walked us to the elevator alone and asked what floor we were on.

'Five,' Lydia said.

'I'm on sixteen, in the penthouse suite. Want to come up?

I shook my head, thinking of Eric in our hotel room waiting for me.

Lydia grabbed my hand. 'Come on, Carly. Eric told Jeff

he didn't care what happened tonight as long as you had a good time.'

I couldn't believe Eric wouldn't care if I had sex with Damien, but I figured he might not mind if I indulged my little fantasy just a bit more. 'Okay.'

Silently we rode the elevator to the sixteenth floor. I expected a wild party to be going on, but the plush suite was silent.

'The rest of the crew is downstairs,' Damien said. 'We have the place to ourselves.'

My heart was hammering my chest and I gave Lydia a panicked look.

Lydia ignored me. 'Damien, Carly is your biggest fan. She thinks you're the sexiest man on the planet. Don't you, Carly?'

I could have killed her. I giggled in embarrassment as we followed Damien 'Yeah, I think you're great. We both do.'

I was so intent on not tripping over my own feet that I didn't realize Damien had led us into the bedroom.

'Really?' Smiling, Damien reached out to me. 'Then I think I need to spend some time with my biggest fans.'

His hand was warm and strong and some of my discomfort faded away as he tugged both Lydia and I down on the king-sized bed. He leaned over and kissed Lydia, a kiss that made Lydia moan softly. She cupped his face in her hand and turned him toward me. I knew I should say no, but I didn't want to. I wanted him to kiss me.

His mouth was warm and wet and kissing him was everything I thought it would be. I whimpered softly as his tongue probed my mouth and I heard him respond with a deep moan. I heard the rasp of a zipper and felt him shift

40

against me. I pulled back and realized Lydia had slipped to her knees between his legs. She held his erection in her hands and looked up at me.

'Isn't it gorgeous, Carly?'

She licked the swollen head softly. 'Oh, and he tastes so good.'

'Suck it,' Damien groaned. 'Suck my dick.'

Lydia obeyed, bobbing her head up and down on his cock, her long blonde hair trailing across Damien's thighs. I had never seen her like this and the thing was, it was turning me on. I could feel myself getting wet as his cock slid in and out of Lydia's mouth.

Pulling me against him, he kissed me. 'I want to fuck you,' he murmured against my lips. 'Can I fuck you?'

'Yes.' I don't know what made me say it, but suddenly I wanted to feel Damien deep inside me. I remembered what Lydia had said about Eric not caring what happened tonight. I clenched my thighs together, feeling my pussy contract. 'I want you to fuck me, Damien,' I whispered.

Lydia slid her mouth from Damien's cock and put her hand on my thigh. I pulled her up and watched as she began undressing. I followed suit, slowly unbuttoning my shirt and slipping it off my shoulders. He cupped my breasts in his hands, teasing my nipples through the cups of my bra. Leaning forward he sucked one hard nipple through the fabric. I moaned and held his head to my chest as Lydia finished stripping.

Damien finished undressing me; first my bra, then my shoes, jeans and panties. I stretched out naked on the bed. 'Your turn. I want you naked, too,' I said, and I couldn't believe that sexy, sultry voice was mine.

He stood up and stripped off his T-shirt. I admired the strong masculine look of his chest and the stark contrast the tattoos made against his skin. His cock was still out of his pants, rigid and glistening from Lydia's mouth. He took off his jeans and shoes and I realized he wasn't wearing underwear. Once naked, he stood at the foot of the bed looking down at me.

'Come here,' I said, reaching a hand out to him.

He took Lydia's hand and helped her onto the bed, then he got between us. 'Who's first?'

'Fuck her,' Lydia said. 'I want to watch.'

He obeyed instantly, taking me in his arms and kissing me, as if sensing how nervous I was. 'Relax,' he whispered against my neck. 'I know how to make you feel good.'

His lips trailed down my body, teasing my nipples with his lips and fingers, sliding his tongue down my ribcage and across my belly, dipping the tip of his tongue into my belly button. I spread my legs around his wide shoulders as he nuzzled my pussy with his lips. I arched my back and raised my hips, silently urging him to lick me.

Instead, he shifted over to Lydia and began licking her pussy. I could feel my own pussy respond to the wet, sucking sounds of Damien's oral caresses, and I wanted it for myself. Lydia pushed her pussy against his mouth and I whimpered softly, longing to do the same.

Suddenly, Damien was between my legs again. He put his hands on the backs of my thighs and pushed my legs toward my chest. I was open, exposed and completely vulnerable to him.

I looked over at Lydia. As she watched, her fingers worked between her thighs, masturbating as she watched Damien go down on me. She tensed, gasped and clamped her thighs around her hand. Her breath came in quick little pants and it was then that I realized she had come. It was

42

one of the sexiest things I'd ever seen and I smiled at her.

She grinned wickedly as she raised her wet fingers to her mouth and licked them. Then, with a gentler touch than Damien, she stroked my nipple with her fingertips. I shivered and moaned. I had never thought of Lydia in a sexual way, but her touch combined with Damien's mouth on my pussy felt incredible. I closed my eyes, imagining it was Eric's fingers stroking my nipples as Damien's tongue slid over my engorged clit and down between my swollen lips, then back up again. Over and over he licked me, teasing my clit, dipping his tongue into my pussy, sucking on my lips.

I felt a similar sucking on my nipple and my eyes flew open. Lydia was licking my nipple in the same rhythm Damien was licking my pussy. I gently pushed Lydia away. 'I can't,' I said. 'It feels good, but I can't.'

'Sorry, I got carried away,' she whispered.

Damien took his mouth off my pussy long enough to say, 'If she doesn't want your mouth, I do.'

Giggling, Lydia slid down the bed and I knew from the wet slurping sounds she was sucking Damien again.

Damien went into overdrive, his mouth working tirelessly on my pussy as he ate me like a piece of ripe fruit, nibbling and sucking until I was whimpering loudly. Then, when I thought I couldn't take any more, his tongue slid across my anus. I gasped and jerked against him and he did it again. Over and over, Damien licked my asshole, pushing the tip of his tongue against the puckered hole and fluttering it as if he was going to fuck me with his tongue. I was whimpering and quivering from the sensation, so aroused and hot I couldn't stand it.

'Here, Damien,' I heard Lydia say, 'I brought it for me, but I think she needs it more.'

I had no idea what she was talking about until I heard the hum of a vibrator and felt Damien press it to my clit. With the vibrator sending shockwaves through my entire body and Damien tongue-fucking my ass, I came. I strained against Damien, clutching at the sheets as I gasped and moaned his name.

Suddenly, he was above me, driving his thick cock into my throbbing pussy. 'Your cunt is so fucking wet,' he gasped.

'Fuck me, fuck me, fuck me,' I whimpered as I clung to him.

Over and over, he thrust into me, his cock filling my pussy as his muscular body pinned me to the bed. I could hear Lydia's soft whimpers and knew she was watching us and touching herself again. I rocked my hips up to meet Damien's thrusts and with an animal-like groan he came. His cock twitched, throbbing inside me as I squeezed my pussy around him, drawing out everything he had to give. I stroked his shoulders and back softly, holding him to me.

'That was incredible,' I whispered.

'In-fucking-credible,' he agreed.

Lydia giggled. 'I wasn't even the one getting fucked and it looked amazing.'

We all laughed quietly, damp and exhausted from the night. All I could think about was telling Eric what had happened.

I felt my eyes flutter closed and the next thing I knew Lydia was shaking me softly. 'C'mon, Carly. The guys are going to be worried about us.'

Damien was asleep and snoring softly. I slipped out of bed and got dressed. Quietly, we left the suite and a very sexy, naked rock star in a tangle of sheets. Lydia started giggling when we got into the elevator.

'What?'

She shook her head. 'I wasn't sure about you, but once you got into it, you really went wild.'

I could feel my cheeks flushing hotly. 'He's incredible.'

'Yeah.'

My heart was hammering in my chest for an entirely different reason when we reached our hotel room. The sun was starting to come up and I expected Eric and Jeff to be asleep, but they were both awake.

'You guys have been gone awhile. Did you have fun?' Jeff asked.

'Hell, yeah,' Lydia said. 'We went to Damien's suite.'

'What happened?' Eric asked.

'She'll tell you later.' Lydia grabbed my hand and pulled me toward the bathroom. 'We need a shower.'

I was so relieved, I didn't even complain when Lydia started undressing me with the bathroom door still open. I expected Eric to say something about Jeff watching me get undressed, but he silently stared as Lydia stripped me naked then removed her own clothes.

Lydia started the shower and pulled me inside with her. The shower door was clear glass and I knew the guys had a perfect view of Lydia and me.

'What are you doing?' I asked as she began soaping my breasts.

'Giving the boys a show.'

'Lydia, I told you I can't do this,' I protested, trying to pull away.

She laughed. 'Don't be silly. We're not going to have sex, we're just going to get them revved up. Once Eric finds out you fucked Damien, he's going to be all over you. This is just to tease him a little longer.'

'Oh.' I couldn't believe the way Lydia's mind worked, but I couldn't deny I was aroused at the thought of fucking Eric so soon after I'd fucked Damien.

I mirrored Lydia's caresses, running the soapy washcloth over her breasts and across her stomach. She seemed to be enjoying herself, posing almost as she let me wash her before returning the favour.

By the time she turned the water off, we were both squeaky clean and wide awake. We wrapped towels around ourselves and stepped out of the steamy shower. I could see Eric and Jeff staring at us like we were dinner and I couldn't help but smile.

'Come here,' Jeff said to Lydia, his voice rough with desire. 'If I don't fuck you now, my dick is going to explode.'

Lydia went to him quickly, stripping off the towel and tugging Jeff's shorts off. 'I need to get fucked hard,' she confessed.

Hesitantly, I sat down next to Eric. 'Well?' I asked softly, trying to ignore Lydia's soft whimpers from the other bed as she climbed on top of Jeff.

'Did you fuck him?'

I looked at him, trying to read his expression. Then I swallowed hard and nodded. 'Yeah.'

'Did you like it?'

I couldn't help it, I smiled. 'Yeah. Are you mad?'

Eric took my hand and put it on his cock. It was rock hard. 'What do you think?'

I pulled the sheet down and stripped off Eric's underwear before stretching out on top of him. 'I want you to fuck me,' I whispered against his jaw. 'I need you inside me.'

I reached down and guided his cock into me, feeling

46

him fill me in a way Damien never could. I rocked on Eric's cock, knowing the way he liked me to move, knowing what it would take to make him explode inside me. He groaned and closed his eyes, his hands cupping and squeezing my breasts as he thrust up into me.

'Oh God, baby, fuck me,' he groaned.

As I rode Eric to an explosive orgasm, I fleetingly wondered if Damien was still asleep and whether Eric would mind visiting the penthouse suite with me later...

The V.I.P.
by Phoebe Grafton

'Hilary Fieldman?'

He was on me almost before I had time to clear customs at Kennedy and step out into the raw New York sunshine.

'Hi! I recognised you from your photographs. I'm Harry, Mr Bernstein's P.A.'

His eyes peeled me like a banana. I hated him straight away. He pumped my hand. His palm was sweaty. Harry was obviously nervous. I began to feel better.

He waved and a limo whispered up. In England it would have been big enough for fare-paying passengers.

The chauffeur, who looked like a retired football pro, and probably doubled as bodyguard, took my hand luggage. When we settled Harry started on his itinerary as if he had been learning it for days. He couldn't sit still. I was right. Harry was a very nervous young man.

'Hey! Your K62zee model has got us all doing flip-ups.'

He stopped as if arrested by a sudden thought. 'Here,' he went on. 'You've had a long journey. Let me pour you a drink.'

The button he pressed changed the whole shape of the car interior as crystal decanters and glasses appeared. They had thought of everything.

Time for a wind-up. 'Fine,' I said. 'I'll have a tequila sunrise.'

He looked as if I'd stolen his pay check.

'Sorry. We're all out of tequila.'

I waved away an alternative offer. We resumed.

'Tell me, Hilary...' He paused. 'You don't mind if I call you Hilary, do you?'

'As a matter of fact, I do...'

He stopped me, blushed, looked confused and crestfallen all at the same time. I was enjoying this. The guy was a creep anyway.

'Sorry, yes of course.' He regained his composure with the sort of speed which belied the fact that he'd probably been used as a doormat for years.

'Tell me, Miss Fieldman, how did you come up with such a simple and effective design?'

I cleared my throat. 'Look...' I began earnestly.

Harry backed off again and offered his hands up in surrender.

'Forget it,' he put in hurriedly, 'I'm strictly a PR man. I leave the micro-chip magic to you technical guys.'

He went back to the script, obviously feeling safer that way.

'The launch is all set.' Harry was breathless. 'I've booked you a suite at the Waldorf. C.J. ...that is, Mr Bernstein, is out of town for the weekend. He's set up a meeting for ten on Monday. In the meantime he wants you to enjoy your stay in New York.'

Harry's collar was too tight and his face got redder as he shot his words out with machine gun rapidity.

He paused for breath. The short skirt on my Armani, black, two-piece, offered him too much thigh.

You certainly are a looker,' he said. 'I mean…'

'Thanks.' I cut him short. He seemed to have enough trouble breathing as it was.

The limo drew up outside the Waldorf. Another retired football pro in uniform took my hand luggage. I stood idly by as Harry whispered instructions and parted with some paper money.

As it pulled away, Harry shouted above the noise of the traffic. 'There are two tickets for a Broadway show at reception. An escort will call for you later.'

I held my breath and waited. Harry didn't let me down.

'Have a nice day.'

Then he was gone.

The Waldorf Astoria I liked. The exterior was very imposing. Art décor at its very best: inside there wasn't a plastic fitting in sight. All chandeliers, mahogany and quiet furnishings; the elevator noiselessly blasted off from the foyer to my penthouse suite.

It was vast. I wandered around those huge rooms feeling lost and not a little lonely. It was a passing mood, for I cheered myself up with a nice hot bath. Fresh and hungry, I waited impatiently to see what happened next.

The phone trilled. It was reception. There was a guest in the foyer. I told them I was available and hung up. This would be my escort. What sort of companion had Harry and his corporation selected? So far I couldn't fault their efforts. If the sales pitch was anything to go by, then my escort should be better than ordinary.

There was a knock on the door. 'Hi,' he said. 'I'm Greg.'

He smiled down at me. I flipped. Greg was strictly centrefold material.

'Hi,' he said again. 'I'm from the escort agency.'

He held out his hand. I took it, then held on to it just in case he vanished as a figment of my imagination. He didn't.

There he stood. Broad, fair, a blue-eyed hunk of a man, the sort I'd always hoped to find under the tree at Christmas.

'I'm here to look after you. If you need anything…anything at all…' he smiled. 'Just ask.'

My hormones began doing press-ups even as he spoke. I cleared my throat. I've been doing that a lot lately.

'Thank you,' I said.

We saw the show. Don't ask me what it was about. I was busy with my own fantasies. Every time Greg turned his head I was made more aware of the attraction of the man.

At dinner, courtesy of C.J., he spoke little but listened a lot. Greg's presence completed that web of intrigue which I was all too happy to be caught up in.

After dinner Greg suggested a night club. The day had been enough for me already. Did his escort duties include accompanying me back to the hotel for a night cap? Indeed they did.

Some time later in the subdued light of the penthouse suite he stood at my side looking out over the city.

Once more I became aware of the overwhelming nearness of him. He swayed towards me and took me in his arms. I shut my eyes. It was Christmas.

Greg pressed his warm, hard body against mine. My body didn't argue. Skilful, knowing fingers found my weakness. I heard myself moan against his ear as my need became all too apparent.

He removed my clothes while my supplicating body offered itself for further attention. Greg cupped the roundness of each breast in his hand. Gently he sucked each nipple into his mouth, pulling it gently between his lips, drawing them to firmness.

He left me for an instant to put the lights out. There still remained sufficient light from the outside to enable me to see him in the shadow. His silhouette melted against mine as he returned to my side.

Strong hands linked beneath my buttocks. I could feel the surge of power through as he lifted me effortlessly to lay me upon the bed. For a brief moment I lay upon the cool sheets looking up at the dark shadow of him. My body quivered in anticipation, thighs parted like serpents' jaws, waiting expectantly to trap this wonderful man inside me.

With relief I listened to his urgency in that darkened room. He quickly discarded his own clothes and leaned over me. His big hands smoothed my inner thighs in torment.

Without further warning he was at the entrance to my contracting vagina. He felt the ease of entry as he stroked the head of his erect organ across its lips, sticky with female arousal.

Then he thrust and I wondrously filled with him, deep inside me.

An evening full of anticipation only left my climax micro-seconds away. So it was that almost the instant he achieved maximum penetration, I felt the bubbling, welling sensation of a shuddering climax begin to build.

I wrapped my legs tightly about him as I felt his own imminent completion. Together we chorused our fulfilment in a duet of ecstatic, breathless sighs.

Soon after, lying in an aura of exhausted contentment, I fell asleep.

Later, in the darkness, while the lights of the city still cast a glow in the room, Greg aroused me again. Even my subconscious must have anticipated his desires. In a frantic, thrusting coupling, our overwhelming hunger for each other found completeness.

When the morning sun woke me I discovered that Greg had gone.

It was but a brief moment of loss and anxiety. I was sure he'd be back.

For a while I lay luxuriating. What does a girl do for laughs in New York on a Saturday? Given the attentions of my escort, thus far, I felt the problems would prove non-existent. In the meantime I indulged myself. A room service breakfast satisfied the inner woman. It was time to clean up the outer woman; even if I was reluctant to rid myself of the exciting man smell of Greg which still clung to me.

The deep, foamy bath proved a further haven for contemplation. It was while I was soaking that I heard the outer door open.

'Is that you Greg?' I called out. It wasn't.

The sliding door opened. 'Hi,' he said. 'I'm Rocky.'

My eyes swept over him. He certainly looked the part.

'Where's Greg?' I enquired, forgetting to look embarrassed.

'He's away today.'

'Oh,' I said a little bitterly. 'He was the Friday shift, was he?'

'It's not like that.' He sounded a little hurt.

I looked up at him. Another centrefold.

Shut up, woman, I told myself. You've scored yourself a matching pair.

In the meantime Rocky was kneeling by the bath. He looked at me intently with his deep, sincere, plain chocolate eyes.

Oh, God, I thought. Here we go again.

It occurred to me that I didn't feel half as shocked at the prospect as I ought.

Rocky spoke. 'I'm here just for you, honey. Anything you want, you just ask.'

I handed him the soap.

If Greg had started a fire in me in the first place, Rocky just poured petrol on it.

The hands that cleansed my willing body were as gentle as those of the previous member of the escort agency. Gentle indeed, although Rocky's were perhaps a little more industrious. He left no part of me untouched – or unwanting!

So smooth was his touch that I felt more anointed than rinsed by the time he'd finished. Dabbing me dry, he stood back to admire his work.

'You sure are a looker, honey.'

Unlike the leering Harry, Rocky's gaze covered my whole body in a warm glow.

I was about to thank him for the compliment, but he started to kiss me. It was about then that my knees turned to jelly. He lifted me from the bath and carried me into the bedroom.

Once he had laid me on the bed, he commenced an erotic feast on my bath-fresh body. His lips burned my inner thigh as they made the swift journey…upwards.

I ripped at his clothing, refusing to be denied my own sensual pleasure. Rocky stopped long enough to release the imprisoned body I now longed to excite. So, in an instant, he stood naked and splendid.

None more aptly named than this man before me. Rock hard, rock solid and rock heavy: he was magnificent.

In the darkness, the sight of Greg's weapon had eluded me. Not so with Rocky. Proud and erect he stood before me…and oh, so huge!

We adjusted our bed positions. While Rocky buried his head between my thighs allowing his tongue to play wicked games, I was likewise busy.

Taking his shaft in both hands to control it, I trailed my lips over the pulsating, velvet head, licking up and down its length, envying the power within its mighty length.

Control fought with impatience and lost as we simultaneously felt the urgency arise within us. A cocktail of emotions, exhilaration, anxiety and warmth swept over me as I lay upon him.

Raising myself above his beautifully developed torso, I straddled him again, easing myself down upon his gorgeous, throbbing shaft.

His voice was raw with passion as I experienced the thick plum of his cock head distending my sex lips to the full.

Slowly I slid down upon him…little by glorious little.

Finally I was totally and inextricably impaled. I could feel the whole length of him inside me.

Our bodies commenced a duel dance of elation as Rocky sought to control my bouncing breasts. The contractions and spasms of the throbbing monster inside alerted me, yet did not prepare me for the final moment.

With a thrust that penetrated to the very centre of my

being, Rocky exploded inside me. Together we celebrated a mutual orgasm in a chorus of torn, gasping whispers.

We lay together, spent and fulfilled.

Rocky and I spent the rest of the day sightseeing. New York is reputed to be the sort of place that girls on their own should avoid. With my powerful and rugged escort at my side however, New York was mine!

We did Fifth Avenue. Saks, Gucci and the rest of them were places I silently vowed to revisit when my Premium Bond came up. Then we called in at Tiffanys. Three floors of porcelain, chic watches and crystal. On my budget I doubt if I could have afforded a cup of coffee let alone a whole breakfast.

Our final call at Tiffanys was the jewellery section. I gazed in wonder at some of the fabulous displays. It was only when, out of the corner of my eye, I caught Rocky's admiring eyes covering my figure that I realized diamonds were not the only friend a girl needs.

Where did the day go? The hours fled and my magic carpet ride ended in the penthouse suite looking out over the city lights. Was it really only twenty-four hours earlier that I'd been standing here with Greg?

It seemed we made love all through the night. Then suddenly it was dawn. Monday was here. Somewhere between waking and dozing I could hear Rocky in the bathroom.

Soon he was gone.

So was I.

The 747 cleared Kennedy and I began dozing again almost before the seat belt sign came up. I stayed awake long enough to dwell on my experiences.

It had certainly been an eventful weekend. As for the Americans…I was a fan!

Admittedly my experience was somewhat restricted, yet it seems they certainly knew how to look after a girl – perhaps with the exception of Harry, but I suppose he'd done his best.

I allowed myself a quiet chuckle at the prospect of the next meeting between C.J. and Harry. I concluded that the big chief would not be best pleased with his PR man. That was the trouble with Harry…too hasty.

Such thoughts faded with a contented sigh. Greg and Rocky! No sir, nobody could fault those Americans for hospitality. I couldn't have had a better time…not even if my name really HAD been Hilary Fieldman!

Dangling by a Thread
by Conrad Lawrence

Date:	Wed, 14 Jun 12:29
From:	Carl@hotferyou.com
Subject:	I'm curious
To:	Amy@silkstockings.net

I'm sitting here grading assignments online so it's easy for me to jump back and forth between my e-mail and work. Aren't you in the middle of a meeting?
  Carl

Date:	Wed, 14 Jun 12:47
From	Amy@silkstockings.net
Subject:	Re: I'm curious
To:	Carl@hotferyou.com

lunch time...and I am emailing during the meeting...keeping me awake.
  Amy

13:22 from Carl@hotferyou.com

Well, I knew you were at lunch and hid myself under the conference table where you are seated. You're wearing a skirt. First, I touch you gently, stroking the backs of your calves, encircling your ankles, placing light kisses on your knees. Then I work my hands up under your skirt, very slowly, deftly. You realize that you are trapped and that I am moving my hands up your thighs so slowly that no one will notice – unless you react. So you sit quietly, struggling to pay attention, to respond – to those in the meeting, not to me.

It takes over five minutes for me to work my hands over the top of your thighs, along the side, until I find the waist-band to your panties and panty hose. My arms are under your skirt past the elbow and I am working and rolling your waistband down over your hip, my face buried between your knees as if they were between the bosoms of a lover. You give in, realizing that trying to stop me is more risky to exposure than giving in. The process of removing your panties takes more than fifteen minutes. My fingers working along the sides of your hips, thighs; over the top of the thighs with quick deft touches; rolling your panties down your legs. When your thighs are exposed, I don't slow as I pull them down your calves, but maintain the same slow plodding diligence in removing them, relishing every moment of contact with you.

You can feel me, my urgency, my hope to open your legs and apply kisses to the inside of your thighs. And...

13:53 from Amy@silkstockings.net

I will not allow for you to seize the moment, and take control of me in any way. I know you cannot be quiet when the pressure is on you. So, I lift the tablecloth higher on my hips to hide what is about to happen.

I take the tip of my shoe and trace it across the floor to figure out where your legs are. I quickly find each leg and follow them to your body. I take the heel of my shoe and gently but firmly push it into your groin area feeling you get bigger. Your hands grab my foot to tell me to stop. I will not listen to you and pull my foot away leaving my shoe in your hand. I quickly feel you getting larger as I slide my foot to your chest to keep you away from me.

Spreading my legs so that you can watch while keeping you at bay, I slide my hand slowly below the table cloth so that I can feel myself getting wet, but stopping you from touching me.

14:12 from Carl@hotferyou.com

I press against your foot, trying to get closer, unable to tear my eyes away from your hand. I have never been able to look away from your hand, its strength and grace always drawing me to you. I am tethered to you by the sight of it covering your sex, deftly touching yourself with slow movements that go beyond exploration. I am torn. I want to be that hand, to press against you, perhaps as it appears, to enter you, to be inside of you with any part of me that I can press into you. But, I also want that hand touching me, encircling my hardening need and urgency with its grace and hold me with its strength, the strength that is your character.

I turn my head, not far enough to lose view of your hand, but to kiss your ankle, my only weapon for softening your defences. Between the tactile persuasion of my tongue on the inside of your ankle and your need to defer some of your attention, I make headway, placing kisses along the inside of your calf and thigh, until I am at your hand, the last barricade between me and you.

I flick at your fingers with my tongue, slipping it up along between the forefinger and middle finger to where they come together in the same way I would like to bring my tongue up between your legs. I press my tongue, working to pry your fingers apart to let me have the barest contact with you. I nuzzle and lightly gnaw at your knuckle in a way that tells you I don't care how many other people are in the room, that I have pulled my rigid need from behind the guard of my zipper and that I want to rise up and enter into you regardless of who is watching. I want to be seen making love to you. I want to be seen with a woman like you.

But, you hold firm and…

14:37 from Amy@silkstockings.net
I know that I have to tell you again…
…NO!!!
I begin to slowly but firmly bend my fingers down and convince you to entwine your fingers in mine. I soften my hold to allow yours to slip between mine. Then, I strike with my nails extended going deep into the flesh at the back of your hand. I know you will not listen and continue.

My mind races on how to get you to stop. How do I continue with this meeting knowing you are there? You will not go away because I am uncomfortable – I have seen you get enjoyment in watching me be uncomfortable in the past. You get aroused in watching me respond to awkward situations. I feel really nervous now and I dig deeper into your skin to say, no!!

Regardless, you pull my hand to the side and begin to twist my wrist just enough to make me release. I realize I do not have the strength against your hand and more of an effort would only make me more uncomfortable within the meeting. So, I loose my nails in your skin, I drop my foot from your chest, and I bend my right knee in front of your face. Slowly, I bring my leg up and over our clasped hands until my legs are open and our hands are under my right thigh. I lean forward. I have you now…your hand and forearm arm caught under my thigh and my leg pushing your body away; my foot finds you. I can feel with my toes how excited you have become, how engorged is your cock.

I know you will not move because you do not want to be found with your member exposed. I take my left hand and slowly rub my inner left thigh; knowing you must watch me now.

15:09 from Carl@hotferyou.com
And I can do nothing more but watch, hoping you will give me more to watch than the torment of what cannot be. I cannot tell where to focus my senses or my sight: Capturing your hand with its long graceful, strong fingers; or do I focus on my painfully hard urgency, so aware of your toes against it?

Not even I can tell if it is the throbbing of my pulse within my member or if I am actually beginning the movement of love. You hold me at that horrid point of almost-but-not-quite climax and I know you know I am there and I cannot tell if what you want is for me to explode all over your foot, ending the only chance I will get to be locked in this close contact with you.

So I watch and watch and fight my climax, relishing that warm hard pain caused by the touch of your toes against me. Your fingers curl and release, caressing the inside of your thigh, then make circles until quietly, I plead 'Please.'

Whoever is speaking falters, unsure if they have heard a voice from under the table.

'Please.'

This time I simply breathe the word against your thigh, then ever so slightly louder,

'Please.'

We both know that I will escalate this unless you do something. I consider, and you consider, the possibility of revealing to the room the extent of desire you invoke in me. You have no choice but to give me something of value to watch. Your hand slides closer to you, deeper between your legs. I press forward and slide back, my hard member sliding along the cleavage between two toes, an inquisition: 'What? What do you want?'

Tell me…

15:48 from Amy@silkstockings.net

I dig my nails into you again as a strong warning that not another peep should come from you. I loosen my grip enough to be comfortable as I lean back in my chair. I feel you pulling your hand away and I dig in again and lean forward. Now, adjusting my weight to hold you in place, I arch my back slightly. I know that I must be comfortable to pleasure myself.

I take my left hand and slowly spread my legs further. I want you to be able to see, but not clearly. I take my hand and make certain that I am somewhat blocking your view. I begin to feel the extreme heat between my legs and know that I want pleasure. My mind races on what I really want.

I want you to watch, I want to tease you, and yet, I want to feel your hands discover me. I want to feel your tongue discover every inch of me. I want to feel submissive to you, your strength, and your manliness…yet I cannot. I am nervous and do not want to release your hand. I must show power and be in control; yet I feel uncomfortable and want to be taken. I want to feel the release of power to you. I am not ready for you to touch me! Yet, I begin to get wet. I know. I feel the aching deep inside of me that causes a sexual frenzy which forces me to satisfy my needs at whatever expense.

I sigh, exhale slowly, breathe in again and exhale, clearing my mind. Pushing out the words of the meeting and opening my mind to feel every last sensation, beginning with my foot. I realize how close you are getting and pull away my foot. I am comfortably located, my legs in a comfortable position.

I reach down further to feel how moist I am. I begin to finger myself letting you watch as I gently rub myself until my finger is glistening from my moisture. I slowly bring my hand to my mouth and taste myself and hear you exhale. I know you must watch and you are frozen in shock that I taste myself in front of everyone. You get bigger with the thought of the taste of me on my lips.

16:05 from Carl@hotferyou.com

Surely you know that my arousal is so hard it hurts, surely that must have been conveyed to you when my rigidity pressed its need against your toes; the sheer urgency vibrating through me. I hold my expression as long as you will allow me contact with you, to feel your arousal through contact with your flesh, not just to know of it by watching. I watch holding on to you. I watch as you bring your hand back to that bleary centre of arousal between your legs, I watch the grace of your hand steering your arousal, hoping you will take it to climax, wishing for all the world that I could supplant that long graceful finger with my tongue. Knowing your climax will be my climax and praying you will not betray us both by circumventing this mutual journey. I vibrate, teetering at the edge of control, knowing that just witnessing your climax I will come without a single thing touching my swollen cock.

I will be quiet as you need, but I convey my mutual level of arousal through kisses and flicks of the tongue inside your thigh. I convey through this oral touch, my desire to want to be a part of your climax, my desire to stand in front of the whole room and let them see as I show you the effect you have on me. And I wonder, if I were to do that, to stand before you hard to the point of bursting, would you want me to just suffer that way as I watch you bring on your own climax or would you prefer me to touch and stroke myself?

It is only the barest hint of intellect that has not been overridden by my passion that holds me under the table telling myself that such things cannot happen...yet.

So I watch your hand, the vehicle of all things graceful in the world as you run it up and down the pursed opening of yourself, sometimes slipping it inside, sometimes lingering at your clit. I hear nothing from you, but can feel your arousal. The waves pass lightly through you and into me, lapping against my psyche like night waves against a boat on a lake. You stop. I hear you answer a question, inconsequential words, not worthy of hearing, so I let them pass and hang at the edge of exploding, both in psyche and physically.

Your hand starts its gesture again and I watch and see...

16:22 from Amy@silkstockings.net
I feel your breath increasing on my thigh and know where you are and how ready you are to explode. I cannot imagine that you have not touched yourself while watching. How could that be? How could you not seek some physical pleasure while you were experiencing visual pleasure? I want you to taste me so I widen my legs fully to allow you to come closer to me. I spread my hands on my inner thighs to communicate to you that I was not going to touch myself and that you must continue for me. I slowly bring my hands around to my hips and then above the table allowing you the freedom of choice, control, and with my complete permission.

17:00 from Carl@hotferyou.com
Your hands move away and I understand the obscurity of this surrender and what it means. I will not abuse it. I leave you the possibility of not being discovered by anyone but me. I reach in along your thighs, feeling every

pore, knowing every possible thing I can of you. I bring my mouth to you, to your lips, those hidden under the table and I kiss, and suckle you, slowly as one kisses a new lover and, eventually, I have my tongue against your clit, and one finger in you, pressing your pleasure, know your climax is due to my foreplay. This is a dangerous journey for me, for I can no longer ignore my need. There is only one way for me to reach my pleasure without betraying you and revealing our tryst. I stroke myself, restraining ejaculation until I can share climax with you.

And you do climax. I hear a stifled noise in your throat, the same as when one stifles a cough. So far we are safe. But you vibrate and the climax ripples through you like an oncoming tsunami and I cannot control myself. I rise up and slide into you regardless of who is watching. I must feel your orgasm in the most intimate way I can, from inside through my own fervent need. I move in, out, with purpose, gauging your climax, still holding back mine until you are finished. And then I pull out and show you in the most rigid of terms the effect you have on me. You gaze at my hard arousal and then up to me. Very quietly I mouth, 'watch'.

I see you taking me in to you with your eyes – I need not even touch myself. I throb and began to climax. You hold your hands cupped below me catching my climax in its pure white honesty And when I am done, I look around. We are alone and I have no idea how long it has been since everyone else departed and you held me in lingering, painful ecstasy. I can only laugh and do what it is I really wanted to do when I had crawled under the table.

I kiss you.

Don't Mind Me
by Landon Dixon

It all started in high school when I had a job as a custodial assistant and stumbled on to a wild sex scene involving my French teacher and the football coach. They were going at it good and hard in her classroom – she on her back on her desk, he standing and pounding her pussy while he held on to her legs – and they didn't notice me as I watched, wide-eyed, from the cracked-open classroom door. I was fascinated by what I saw, and how I felt seeing it, and, needless to say, I had my own mess to clean up by the time the two sex-crazed educators finished off their lesson for that night. From then on, voyeurism became an obsession with me.

My current apartment is on the fifth floor of a two-tower complex, which gives me a sweeping vista of the apartments directly across and above and below mine. I own a pair of binoculars and a telescope, of course, and have a pair of night-vision goggles on order. I work two jobs: window washer during the short, mild winter, and lifeguard at a hotel-resort that caters to newlyweds during the long, hot summer. My hobbies include astronomy and bird watching, and I'm a huge fan of virtually all spectator sports, so you get the picture. Don't get me wrong, I like to do it as much as the next guy, but, frankly, I like to watch even more, because you never know just what you're going to see when the juices start flowing.

For example, shortly after I moved into my apartment, I was calibrating my binoculars on the adjacent building late one Friday night, restlessly sweeping back and forth, up and down, when I located a scene that held real promise – two guys and a girl sitting on a couch passing around a joint. One of the tricks to successful voyeurism, as opposed to aimless scanning, is to locate a situation that has potential and then stick with it, patiently watch it unfold. My instincts, honed over years of eye-popping observation, plus the fact that the girl was openly frenching one of the guys, told me that I had deliberately stumbled onto something well worth watching.

So, I set the binoculars on their tripod and focused in on the developing male-male-female get-together. Then I quickly stripped off the only thing I was wearing – a pair of shorts – and started stroking my ever-ready rod. And, lo and behold, as I sat in front of my darkened window, my eyes glued to the sex-finders, my hand tugging on my rock-hard cock with practiced ease, the girl extracted her long tongue from her friend's mouth, slid off the couch, and proceeded to do an awkward striptease for us three horny guys. She stumbled around a lot, knocked over a lava lamp and some bottles, but somehow managed to peel off her tight, purple top and faded blue jeans.

She wasn't wearing any underwear, and her big tits hung loose and natural, her pussy neatly shaved except for a reverse triangle of fur just above her slick opening. She was a natural blonde, and her lush body was tanned golden brown. I increased the torque on my cock as I peered through the binoculars, as the uninhibited sweet young thing swayed to some music that probably only she could hear, cupped her breasts and rolled her mocha nipples between her fingers. Then she beckoned the two fellows forward with her finger. They sprang up off the couch, shed their garments like they were on fire, and latched on to her tits. She threw her head back and her mouth broke open, her golden hair cascading down her back as the men fed hungrily on her boobs. They clutched and squeezed a tit apiece, suckled the blonde babe's engorged nipples.

I'd finally hit the sexual motherlode after five nights of fruitless searching, and I gripped my dick and fisted happily as I witnessed the heated three-way from afar. Sweat prickled my forehead and rolled down into my eyes, but I blinked it away, never once taking my steely glare off the scene unfolding in my 40X field of vision. The seasoned voyeur knows that a concentrated stare is a must if he wants to get full value for his endless hours of looking.

After getting her huge tits licked and sucked and fondled for a good long while, the sexed-up blonde dropped to her knees and grabbed a cock in each hand. She stroked the guys' hard-ons, glancing appreciatively from one stiffy to the other, then up at her boyfriends. She smiled a wicked, knowing smile and popped one of the cocks into her mouth, sucked on it for a moment, and then partially swallowed the other prick. She bobbed her pretty head back and forth between the two cocks, sucking expertly on each in turn, polishing one slimy rod with her hand while she vacuumed the other one with her mouth. I almost blew my load when she jammed both of them into her mouth at once. But, again, a veteran voyeur doesn't spill his seed until he's seen all there is to see.

71

The two simultaneously cock-sucked guys hung on to each other's shoulders, hung on for dear life as that sun-burnished babe crammed both of their dicks into her stretched-out mouth and sucked on them. Her cheeks and nostrils billowed in and out as she blew the two swollen cocks at the same time, until she finally disgorged her boy-toys and got back to her feet. She pushed one of the guys down onto the couch and climbed on top of him, steered his straining member into her pussy. And as he quickly began sliding his cock in and out of her cunt, she reached back and spread her butt cheeks, inviting the second dude to shove his schlong up her ass.

'Holy shit!' I mumbled to myself, briefly breaking the voyeur code of silence.

The standing guy thoroughly spit-lubed his cock and his shared gal's bunghole, and then climbed into position and eased his inflamed prick into her tight behind. From there, the already hot action turned scorching, and I buffed my cock and pinched my nipples with reckless abandon as blondie got vigorously banged from front and rear. I knew that the blistering tableau couldn't last for long, and, sure enough, the guy on the bottom churning his cock back and forth in the girl's gash suddenly opened his mouth and let out a roar that I could almost hear, and feel, and came in her pussy.

His body shook as he gripped the hottie's slim waist and shot spunk deep inside of her, and the guy hammering on her back door promptly lost it as well. He ass-slammed her in a frenzy, then was jolted repeatedly by orgasm. And the gorgeous girl, who was the cause of all the coming, who was getting her sex-holes filled to overflowing with hot, sticky cream, was overcome herself, and her glistening body quivered uncontrollably as she came right along with her men. I made it a four-for-four, shooting sperm all over my hardwood floor as I ogled the three-way meltdown. The guys with the fleshy cunt and butt plugs came and came hard, as did the girl getting plugged, as did I. And that's what it was all about, after all – mutual satisfaction.

Another time, when I was working my summer job at the lake, I came across two newlyweds enjoying the great outdoors and each other. I'd taken the job at the wilderness hotel-resort for just this purpose, of course – no two people on the face of the earth are hornier than newlyweds on their honeymoon – and I'd been richly rewarded for my foresight. As any good voyeur worth his salty discharge knows, by increasing the potential for sexual situations, you increase your actual sexual sightings.

In this case, I'd gone for a walk in the pristine woods that surrounded the lodge and adjacent cabins. Most of the cabin windows were securely draped shut, so I followed one of the hiking trails that led to a smaller lake, a more secluded beach, to the west. I'd gone only half a mile or so, stealthily as usual, when I heard the faint but unmistakable gruntings and groanings of a young couple in heat.

I tip-toed off the beaten cedar chip path and through the pine and birch trees until I came to a slight clearing in the dense forest. In the middle of this grassy clearing, on a beach towel that hadn't made it all the way to the beach, were an amorous recent bride and groom sixty-nining each other. I swallowed my excitement and concealed myself in the brush, swiftly pulled down my shorts and grabbed up my cock. The cool, pine-scented air felt great on my hard

73

dick, my pumping fist even better.

'Yes! God, yes! Eat me, Gavin!' the twenty-something, flat-on-her-back honeymooner cried as her eager beaver husband lapped at her cunny. She writhed around on the blanket like a woman possessed as she got tongue-lashed, her long, black hair whipping back and forth across her flushed face. Then she gripped her beau's rigid cock and guided it into her anxious-to-please mouth.

'Fuck, yeah, Jan!' the blushing boy hollered, lifting his face out of his wife's pussy as she swirled her thick, pink tongue all over his cockhead.

Now this was the wild kingdom at its wildest, I thought gleefully, as I spat into my hand and greased up my pole. Rays of hot sunlight stabbed through the green canopy, providing me with a brilliant view of the orally obsessed lovers.

'Suck me, Jan,' Gavin groaned, his eyes closed. 'Suck my cock, baby.' Jan swabbed all around her man's mushroomed cocktop, and then slid his dickhead into her mouth and started sucking, craning her neck to swallow more and more of the lucky stiff's cock into her warm, wet mouth. Gavin pumped his hips up and down, desperate to fill his betrothed's mouth with the entire impressive length of his meat, as he went back to work on Jan's cunt.

I stole a quick glance around to ensure that I was the only animal of the forest watching the high-intensity erotic coupling, and then I fixed my gaze squarely back on to the young lovers. Gavin gripped Jan's thighs and buried his hardened tongue into her pussy, fucking her with his slippery pink spear. She let out a cock-muffled moan that travelled clear through the shaking guy's body, then applied even deeper suction to Gavin's shaft.

I pulled on my own straining dick with one hand while

I cupped and juggled my balls with the other, staring in wonderment at the oral antics taking place only a few yards away from me in that outdoor playground. I soon felt a tell-tale tightening of the balls signalling imminent blast-off. But even before I could douse the foliage with protein, Gavin pressed Jan's swollen clit between his fingers and energetically sucked on it – causing the overwhelmed girl to convulse with orgasm.

My cock erupted and I showered the greenery with spunk as Jan's slim body quivered with ecstasy. Her soul mate sucked all the harder on her clit as she squirmed beneath him, coated his lips and chin with honey, and then he too groaned and I could tell that he was shooting semen down his beloved's throat – an impression that was confirmed when gooey sperm oozed out of the corners of Jan's cock-stuffed mouth.

I came hard and long as the wind whispered through the tall trees and the blazing sun beat down on the gratified newlyweds, marking my territory in the wordless way of the voyeur. And I stuck around as the sexy pair cuddled for awhile, their naked young bodies glistening with sweat. I was rewarded for my patience when Jan eased herself down on Gavin's re-hardened cock and rode the both of them, and me, to another spectacular orgasm.

My window-washing job also provides me with occasional voyeur action – especially when I'm cleaning the glass on an apartment building or hotel. However, when I'm squeegeeing the grime off an office building during the course of a busy business day, there's usually little to see except for a woman adjusting her bra, or maybe, if I'm lucky, changing into sports or evening wear in her office. So, what I often do is return to an office tower worksite after dark, long after the working day has ended, and lower myself over the ledge and down the side of the building in search of some distinctly unprofessional activity.

One night, as I winched down a fifty-storey corporate headquarters, I spied with my very keen eye a couple of women talking to each other in a large, otherwise empty boardroom – a couple of very attractive women. The older of the two, who looked to be around forty, had glasses, and her lustrous brown hair was pulled back into a short ponytail. She was wearing a no-nonsense white blouse and black skirt. The other woman appeared to be in her early twenties, a petite girl with short, red hair, clad in a body-moulding grey dress. And as I dangled outside the brightly-lit window that showed off the gleaming boardroom table and the two women in earnest conversation, I almost broke out in a cheer when the mature babe suddenly grabbed the redhead in her arms and kissed her full on the lips, thus ending their confab.

The redhead was clearly stunned, unsure of how to respond, but then she did the right thing and wrapped her arms around the other woman and reciprocated with her lips. My boner almost smashed in the window, and I thanked the cold, starry heavens for my good fortune in finding such a heated view after only three hours of searching. I glared intently at the burgeoning non-business relationship as it blossomed into full-blown lust.

The brunette tore off her glasses, grabbed the younger woman's head in her hands, and mashed her mouth against her colleague's mouth, kissing her wildly. She painted the girl's glossy lips with her swirling tongue, then shoved it inside the redhead's open mouth. The two corporate babes frenched excitedly as I whipped out my pecker, teetering dangerously on the wooden platform as I did so.

The brunette broke mouth-to-mouth contact long enough to kiss and lick and bite her way up and down the other woman's slender neck, her wet tongue travelling all over the girl's soft throat, and then across her lips again. The redhead responded by tearing open her new-found lover's blouse, spraying buttons everywhere. Then she popped the brunette's bra, releasing the woman's over-sized tits to both of our astonished sets of eyes.

The bare-chested lady had a gorgeous set of jugs, large and round, capped by jutting, pink nipples that begged to be sucked. The lust-crazed redhead wasted little time in going to work on those luscious tits – teasing the swollen nipples with her tongue, vacuuming one distended nip into her mouth and sucking on it, then doing the same with the other bud. The breast-assaulted babe's mouth fell open and her head lolled back as her engorged nipples were lightly bitten and roughly sucked, her tits squeezed and licked. She somehow managed to unhook her skirt, and then reluctantly pushed her ardent lover back and helped the girl strip off her own dress and bra and panties, till the two career women were both nude and lewd, their curvaceous bodies shining under the florescent lights.

My breath fogged up the window as I pressed my face to the glass and furiously jacked my cock. The two babes clambered onto the boardroom table, sending water bottles and business papers sailing off into oblivion as they cleared a spot for themselves on that varnished slab of wood. They kissed and frenched some more, the redhead on her back, the brunette on top of her, their tits pressed heatedly together. Then the older woman positioned herself so that her furry snatch was rubbing up against her sex partner's pussy.

I stared and stroked as the two beautiful women ground their glistening slits together. The redhead gripped the brunette's boobs and fondled and kneaded them, while the brunette desperately fucked her young lover with her cunt. And, this time, I got so caught up in the action that I didn't even try to synchronize my orgasm with those of the ones I was watching. The cool night air on my superheated cock, my precarious position dangling from a downtown skyscraper, and the triple X sight of those vixens cunt-pumping each other all conspired to drive me to the spurting point even quicker than normal, and I coated the tinted glass with cum as I kept my eyeballs peeled on the lesbian cunt grind.

The brunette's undulating body suddenly shook with orgasmic tremors, as the wet, hot pussy friction built to the boiling point and beyond, and the redhead's mouth gaped open in a silent scream as she too was consumed by ecstasy. I pumped jizz for as long as I could, then shakily zipped up and ascended back to the roof, leaving a token of my appreciation on the side of that seemingly staid office tower.

I don't get all of my jollies from voyeurism, mind you, but when I am actually with a woman, I make sure that all the shades are up and curtains open and lights on, just in case there's another of my ilk lurking outside. Every once in awhile you have to give something back to the community, after all.

Favourite Flight
by N. Vasco

I used to hate flying. Bad food, pressure in your ears, long waits at the terminal and now, since September 11th things have only got worse. But I say used to because of what happened on a business trip two weeks ago.

I was at the airport waiting for a tram to take me to my gate. It was midnight, I hadn't bathed for over twelve hours and my mouth tasted like something had died in it.

Suddenly, I detected the scent of a woman's perfume and saw a gorgeous, exotic beauty step onto the platform. Her fitted, knee-length skirt hugged a pleasantly curvy ass and revealed a pair of shapely calves. Black stiletto heels graced her dainty feet, not too high but enough to make my growing erection tug at my pants. The twin mounds of her breasts filled her short little jacket very nicely. Even the cute blue cap on her lustrous black hair looked sexy: the black name tag pinned to her jacket said her name was Tia. I stared long enough to make her look at me.

Her make-up reminded me of an Egyptian queen, complementing her almond-shaped eyes and high cheekbones. She gave me a dazzling smile, her white teeth contrasting dramatically with her red lips. I wanted to go over and say hi but remembered my foul breath. She seemed to expect an introduction but I just nodded and went into the men's room. Luckily it was on my side. I brushed my teeth quickly (you have to be prepared on these business trips) stepped back outside and saw the tram had arrived. It was one of those glass-walled jobs you had to stand in. I'd half expected her to be inside that thing waiting for me. Alas, she was not. It was empty.

You have to wonder how many opportunities are lost due to lack of breath mints.

I sighed, felt myself go limp inside my pants and stepped aboard. To make matters worse, the tram went in the opposite direction to the one I wanted to go. I had to go three terminals down until it started back to the far end of the airport before we reached the place where I'd first got on.

I was reading my paper when I smelled that perfume again and heard the tap of high heels. I looked up. Tia stepped inside but she wasn't alone. Another exotic beauty in a similar uniform followed her in. My eyes feasted on a pair of swaying hips and full, round bottoms heading for the front of the tram.

The other girl had a paler complexion and slanted eyes but was just as sexy as Tia. I gave them quick glances as they talked, even catching a friendly smile from Tia and a few giggles from Faun (the other girl's name I learned by virtue of her lapel tag). I couldn't help but notice how close they stood to each other as they spoke and how Faun kept stroking Tia's arm in a very tender manner. The thought of these two lovelies in a more intimate relationship made me excited again and when Tia caught my stare she gave me a playful smile before leaning close to Faun. Occasionally she stroked her waist as they talked.

Needless to say, my imagination all but took off. I almost expected them to start kissing but was disappointed when the tram stopped at my terminal, putting the little show I was enjoying to a halt.

Hope returned when both women passed me as I made my way to the check-in line. Tia glanced at the ticket in my hand and gave me a quick but provocative smile. I realized the logo on her cap matched the one on my ticket.

While waiting at the passenger line I observed the two lovelies making for the crew entrance. I especially watched Tia, loving the way she walked on those thin heels. My heart all but leapt when she gave me a quick wave and stepped inside.

When I got to the plane Faun was standing there. Flashing her pretty smile, she examined my ticket and frowned.

'I'm sorry, you requested non-smoking but the only section is back in coach.'

Her coy look made me think something was up. She looked behind me over my shoulder.

'Tia, could you help me?'

That perfume came back. I turned and stared right into Tia's sexy black eyes. She took the ticket from Faun and without looking at it said 'My colleague's right, this is a smoker's flight. Non-smoking section is back in coach. Would you mind sitting alone back there?'

Tia turned and walked down the aisle, offering me the sight of her swaying hips. I followed her past the randomly occupied seats (it was a red-eye flight) towards the back, all the while admiring the outline of what I knew were a pair of thong panties underneath her tight blue skirt. She stopped, turned and gracefully pointed the seat out for me.

We were alone in the coach section.

'Do you mind sitting by yourself?'

'No. Not at all.'

I had to squeeze past her to get to my seat, a pleasurable experience as it turned out. I could've sworn I felt her nipples glide across my chest through our clothes.

'You can put your carry on up here.' She indicated the overhead locker and reached up. The hem of her skirt rode up exposing a set of black lacy garters on each thigh.

She noticed my eyes feasting on her shapely legs and smiled.

'I've always preferred stockings over pantyhose,' she said while adjusting her skirt. 'They make me feel so…free.'

The captain's voice over the intercom interrupted our mutual amusement.

Tia sighed and promised she'd return after the plane took off.

I didn't hear any ringing in my ears or feel the pressure of the take-off. I was too busy trying to guess what colour thong she wore under her skirt.

As soon as the seat belt sign turned off I took out my lap-top, turned it on and began to catch up on my work. I was so caught up I didn't hear the sound of a pushcart coming down the aisle or sense anyone standing near me until I heard a slight, feminine cough.

It was Faun, leaning next to a drink cart in a very casual manner. She had taken off her jacket, revealing the pretty white blouse that was a standard for the airline.

She gave me a smile and offered me a drink. I accepted.

'Not too lonely back here? she said, while glancing around the empty section.

Before I could answer she undid the top two buttons of

her blouse and fanned herself.

'There's a little problem with the A/C back here. It usually gets pretty hot.' I took a nervous sip from my drink as she hitched up her skirt ever so slightly and adjusted the lacy black garters that contrasted nicely against her smooth, creamy thighs.

'I got these yesterday. Don't you think they're pretty?'

'Yes, I do. As a matter of fact, I couldn't help but notice that Tia wears the same kind.'

She stood up, straightened her skirt, grabbed the handles as if to leave and looked me straight in the eye.

'You're right. Tia and I share a lot of things. It's what friends do, don't you agree?' She threw me a parting glance before leaving and said 'Tia will be here later with your dinner. I hope you enjoy it.'

I couldn't help feeling I had passed some sort of test.

Later, that unmistakable scent caressed my nostrils. Tia entered with the dinner cart and I instantly noticed she wasn't wearing a bra. I admired her dark ample nipples poking through the white fabric.

She undid the two buttons of her blouse and said 'I hope you don't mind, but it gets awfully hot on these flights sometimes.'

'I was told that.'

She gave me an inviting smile and placed a decent looking portion of sushi on my tray. By now the scent of her perfume had covered me in an erotic haze. I looked straight in her eyes as she set down a pair of chopsticks, a teapot and a small bowl.

'This is a generous portion,' I said 'Would you like to share it with me?'

Without a word she sat down, crossed her beautiful legs in a very sexy manner, again revealing her lacy garters.

She brushed my hand aside when I reached for the teapot, shaking her head in a playful manner as she poured the hot liquid into the bowl.

I picked up the bowl, looked at her and said 'An old-fashioned girl in high heels, what could be better?'

We both giggled. My movements caused the bowl to slip from my hands and spill the hot fluid on my chest. Before I could gasp Tia instantly pulled out a cool wash cloth and began wiping my chest. Any thought of pain was instantly removed. She leaned close enough to press her nipples on my arm. I told her I was okay but she insisted I unbutton my shirt.

'I have to check for burns,' she replied and before I knew it, her deft hands had most of my chest exposed. Her noble fingers glided over my bare skin before she pressed her palm against my chest, leaned close and commented how fast my heart was beating.

That was it. I gave Tia a light kiss on her beautiful lips and told her she was the reason. She smiled, took my hands and pressed them between her sexy breasts. I could feel her heart racing as fast as mine. She kissed me, this time opening her lips and probing my mouth with her tongue.

Her breath tasted like honey. She gasped as I ran my other hand over her stockings until I reached the bare skin of her thigh. She responded by gently scratching my nipples with her beautiful red nails. I cupped her breasts. Her nipples turned hard against my palms. She stood up, unzipped her skirt and turned to reveal a tiny black thong dividing her luscious buttocks. After removing her blouse, she began stroking her bare, tanned breasts and those lovely dark nipples. She murmured with pleasure, then eyeing me thoughtfully, pushed back her seat, turned her back to me and crouched on it. I had a full and glorious view of her lovely ass. It was more than I could take. I stood behind her, cupped both her cheeks with the palm of my hand and slipped my finger in her wet, inviting pussy. She gasped with delight as I knelt, pushed her thong aside and began feasting on her loins. Her moans grew louder as I licked and sucked her lips and willing clit. My tongue found the opening of her pussy. I probed it deep and heard her say 'Yes' over and over. Soon my face was covered with her sweet juices. I moistened my index finger in her wet hole and probed her tight little anus while licking her crotch.

A minute later she arched her back and quivered one last time, her juices covering my face and coating the inside of my mouth. I got up, unzipped my pants and whipped out my bulging cock. She looked back at the hard meat in my hands, grabbed it and slipped it inside her pussy.

Her tight, cherry walls surrounded my cock, as I slid inside her body. She gasped again, swayed her hips back and forth as I started pumping. I leaned back and inserted my finger in her ass again.

That was it.

The tight space got even tighter. I began to moan, almost ready to come. Tia looked at me and said 'Please...I want you to come in my mouth!' I barely nodded and whipped out my cock just as she turned and took it deep inside her throat. It was my turn to shout. She sucked me until I had to give in. My come gushed into her mouth. I collapsed into the next seat.

But she wasn't finished with me yet. Wrapping her leg around me, the silky black nylons making rasping noises around my hips, she said 'That was very nice. I never had my anus stimulated like that. Would you like to go to my place after we land and have anal sex? It'll be my first time.'

'Sure.' I said.

She started playing with my nipples and the pensive look on her pretty face made me ask her what was on her mind.

'Faun's never had anal sex either. Maybe we could have a threesome?'

Like I said, I used to hate flying.

Coffee Break
by Teresa Joseph

Down on her knees like a good little bitch in the changing cubicle of 'Gilbert & Sons Quality Men's Wear', the sexy young sales assistant sucked and blew for all she was worth, taking the whole length of the customer's cock down the back of her throat, desperate to swallow his spunk. Having bought more than a dozen suits from the company because of their excellent customer service, the man was more than willing to give her exactly what she desired.

After more than twenty years of dwindling profits and falling sales, the manager of Gilbert & Sons had hit upon the perfect sales tactic, something that would allow them to finally compete with the cut-price competition and earn him his much coveted promotion. And so, hiring a dozen sexy young university graduates for their looks rather than for their talent, he set himself the task of moulding them into the perfect sales force and had succeeded beyond his wildest dreams.

At first of course he had tried to use a bonus system, giving each girl £100 for every suit she sold. And on top of that, he also introduced an 'anything goes' sales policy to make it clear that he didn't care what each girl did as long as she sold a suit. But while this was more than enough incentive for the girls to wear short skirts and flirt with the customers, it still cut very deeply into the company's profits and he was certain that they could do more.

Like all the best ideas of course, the answer to this problem came to him like a bolt out of the blue one day during the morning coffee break as all twelve girls sat comfortably in the staff room upstairs.

This was the moment that they all looked forward to all day: a chance to relax and unwind.

'Well, since they look forward to it so much already,' he grinned sadistically, 'maybe I could make them look forward to it even more.'

Of course, at times like this it's important to have an unscrupulous friend who just happens to be the head of pharmaceutical research at a major drugs company. And since Mr Johnson just happened to have such a friend, the next day when he treated all of the female staff to a *special* cup of coffee, it was the most wonderful experience of their young lives.

'Please, Mr Johnson!' They begged emphatically having become completely addicted to the coffee after the very first sip and now willing to do anything for another single drop. 'Please can you make us another cup of coffee! We'll do anything you want! Absolutely anything at all!'

For one brief exciting moment, the thought of using these sexy young caffeine addicts as his own personal harem loomed large in the manager's mind. But his sales figures were his priority, and so somehow managing the impossible feat of keeping his cock in his trousers while a dozen gorgeous and willing girls pleaded with him to let them satisfy his every perverted desire, Mr Johnson put forward his new sales policy feeling certain that his assistants would agree.

'What I want you all to do is to *sell suits*.' He stated rather firmly, gently slipping his hand up Lydia's tiny pencil skirt and smiling at just how wet and willing her pussy had become.

Needless to say, the manager was delighted with this unexpected turn of events, since while he had been promised that this new chemical was not only absolutely addictive to women but also guaranteed to turn them into horny, submissive slave girls, he'd never dreamed that it could ever be this powerful. But despite his reservations, with a single wave of his hand he made all twelve girls go down on their knees like obedient puppies before continuing to speak.

'Since you want coffee and I want you to sell suits, why don't we alter the bonus system so that for every suit you sell, I give you a cup of coffee instead of £100?'

The girls agreed so vehemently that it almost looked as if they were going to explode. After all, what was a hundred measly pounds compared to another deliciously addictive drop? And so rising back up to their feet, feeling more motivated than ever to sell as much as they possibly could, they asked Mr Johnson's permission to leave and waited patiently for his reply.

'Off you go then, girls'' he said in a particularly paternal tone of voice. 'And remember, it doesn't matter what you do, as long as you make a sale.'

Of course, one of the reasons why Mr Johnson had insisted that the chemical should induce submissive sexual obedience in his staff as well as a powerful addiction was that, while a dozen horny sex toys who were willing to fuck to make a sale would sell suits by the truckload, a dozen violent addicts who were willing to kill each other to make a sale would quickly land him in prison.

Despite his friend's reassurances however, Mr Johnson was still terrified that when a customer walked in through the front door, the girls would all be so desperate for a *bonus* that they would fight each other for the right to make the sale. But nevertheless, when a man did finally walk into the shop and ask Jennifer to help him pick out a dinner jacket, while the other girls were obviously heartbroken, they didn't even say a word.

'This one will make you look *really* handsome,' panted Jennifer, hardly able to decide what it was that she wanted more: another cup of delicious coffee or to be fucked by this man until she died of pleasure.

'Are you sure?' he queried thoughtfully. 'I mean, it *is* very nice, but it's £700.'

'Don't worry about that,' she purred, wrapping her arms around his body and giving him a long lustful kiss on the lips. 'Why don't I help you try it on and I'm sure you'll decide that it's worth the money.'

Jennifer's less than subtle body language soon made it clear what he could expect if he decided to try on the suit. And so, following the helpful assistant through into the cubicle and grunting with pleasure as she knelt down to suck his swollen cock, it wasn't long before he decided that she was worth two suits at that price.

Having greedily swallowed his hot sticky spunk, the shop assistant then stripped completely naked apart from her stiletto heels as the customer tried on his suit, desperate to show off her firm tanned curves, to be fucked unconscious and to savour another serving of Mr

Johnson's special blend

'If you wear a suit like that, the ladies will be begging you to fuck them in the arse,' she panted prophetically, 'assuming the position' against the cubicle wall and spreading her legs as wide as she could. 'Please fuck my arsehole! Please fuck me really hard!'

And with the sight of her gorgeous willing body making him hornier than he could possibly imagine, after such a satisfying blowjob, he effortlessly slipped his massive hard-on between the cheeks of her peachy rump and slipped it so deep into her arsehole that the whole shop heard her moan.

After five minutes of deep, thrusting penetration, having shot a second load so deep inside Jennifer that she could actually feel its warmth inside her tummy, the customer then happily announced that he would buy the dinner jacket.

She was so delighted that she didn't even bother to put her clothes back on! And hurrying over to the till as fast as her well-fucked arsehole would allow, she took the £700, popped the suit in a bag, said 'Have a nice day' and ran upstairs for her second coffee break before he had even left the shop.

'Do you have to go right now?' asked Angela, before the customer had a chance to leave, desperate to make a sale of her own and not sure if she could wait for another customer to walk in. 'Maybe I could show you some other suits that would be perfect for your frame.'

At first of course the man wasn't sure whether to accept her offer or to just politely walk away. After all, there's only so much that a man's wallet, and testicles, can take in one day. But as the voluptuous 'Jessica Rabbit' look-a-like slowly unbuttoned her white cotton blouse, sensually wrapped her arms around him and gave him a long amorous kiss, he quickly decided that this was the day to invest in a brand new wardrobe.

Upstairs in the staff room meanwhile, kneeling naked on the floor like an obedient little bitch, Jennifer licked her lips with anticipation as Mr Johnson waited for the kettle to boil.

Her mouth was watering almost as much as her pussy as she remembered the taste of her very first sip. And as the manager poured the boiling water into the cup and the room was filled with the delicious aroma, Jennifer became so desperate that she literally began to beg for her coffee like a well-trained bitch on heat.

'You're a good little girl, aren't you, darling,' teased Mr Johnson, unable to resist the urge to smile as he handed his assistant the steaming cup and watched her greedily drink up every drop, even licking the empty mug and sniffing as deeply as she could to savour the addictive aroma. 'If you get back to work right away then I'm sure that I'll be able to make you another cup or two.'

Downstairs meanwhile, having long since bared her breasts and pussy, Angela was groaning with ecstasy as the customer fucked her right there in the middle of the shop, doing everything she could to earn her second cup of the day.

'Fuck me really hard, sir! Fuck me really hard,' she panted, almost passing out with orgasm as the cock thrust inside her pussy.

If only Mr Johnson had rewarded her there and then, pouring the coffee into her mouth as the well-hung man fucked her into another incarnation, then this would have been the most wonderful moment in her life.

Still feeling as if his cock was buried hilt deep inside

her arsehole as she slowly made her way back downstairs, still as naked as a stripper and savouring her two most recent addictive experiences, Jennifer was the only other woman in the room to know just how satisfying the customer's cock really was. But, denied the pleasure of his throbbing member and the caffeinated ecstasy that it would undoubtedly bring, as the ten other shop girls noticed the smell of coffee on Jennifer's breath, it wasn't long before the naked girl found out how satisfying a lesbian kiss could be as well.

'You smell *so good*,' moaned Lydia, erotically lapping at Jennifer's lips and at the small trickle of coffee that had trickled between her breasts. 'Can you still taste the coffee on your tongue?'

'Oh yes,' groaned the naked shop girl. 'Would you like to share?'

A few moments later, the two women were kissing so deeply that anyone who passed at that moment would definitely have got the wrong idea. And having shared as much as she could with the sexy young brunette, Jennifer gladly kissed all of the other girls in turn.

Even Angela, still lying on the floor with her arms and legs wrapped tightly round the man who was pumping his cock inside her, received another taste of what was to come. And while it wasn't as good as being able to drink when being fucked, Jennifer's coffee-flavoured lips soon had the voluptuous redhead coming so hard that the customer had no choice except to follow suit.

'*Oooohhh…thank you sir.*' She moaned with blissful satisfaction. 'Would you like to take the grey suit or the navy blue?'

'I think that you've convinced me to take both,' smiled

the customer, making Angela squeal with such ecstatic delight that no one in the room could help but feel jealous of her success.

Two cups of coffee and a spectacular fuck! It was like a dream come true. And dashing upstairs to receive her reward with her breasts still bared, the cum still dripping from her pussy and leaving Lydia to complete the sale, she went down on her knees like a good little bitch and waited for the kettle to boil.

Downstairs meanwhile, Lydia was doing everything she could to join her colleague, short of buying a suit for herself. The aroma of Angela's delicious reward drifted downstairs and made the girls more desperate than ever.

'Would you maybe like to buy two of each suit?' she suggested as she climbed up onto the counter and spread her legs to reveal her smooth shaven pussy.

And while the customer knew that his bank manager would never forgive him, soon he went down on his knees to lick Lydia's gorgeous slit.

Thankfully for the poor exhausted customer of course, as soon as he had bought another suit from Lydia, another customer walked in and asked Fiona for assistance. And while he promised himself that he would come back next pay day, his poor exhausted cock and depleted wallet insisted that he leave while he still could.

'Do you hang to the left or to the right, sir?' asked Fiona as Lydia ran upstairs, casually unzipping the new customer's fly, going down on her knees and taking every inch of his cock down the back of her throat. 'Oh yes, I *definitely* think we can find a suit to fit this gorgeous frame.'

Later that night after closing time, having eagerly

served every customer to the best of their ability, the twelve shop girls cleaned the shop from top to bottom, totalled up the receipts and restocked the shop in absolutely record time. And having been rewarded with an extra-strong cup of Mr Johnson's special blend, they all went home to wait and yearn for the next working day to dawn.

Too addicted to sleep for very long, the twelve girls each decided to focus all of their efforts on making themselves as enticing as possible to make sure that they made a sale. And so shaving their pussies completely smooth and dressing up in stockings, suspenders and microscopic skirts with no knickers of any kind, each girl made sure that, when the shop opened at nine, no man who passed the window would be able to resist going inside.

Of course, a men's clothing retailer staffed by women who looked like they belonged in a lap-dancing club did have its drawbacks, a fact that was most obviously illustrated by a visit from a pair of pretty young WPCs who had come to make sure that everything was above board.

It was clear from the expression on the police officers' faces as they inspected the premises that they were both appalled and disgusted by the way these women were flaunting their bodies in public. But then again, once Mr Johnson had invited them upstairs and made a cup of coffee for each of them, their attitudes towards the staff's behaviour became very positive indeed.

'Would...would you like us to recommend your shop to all of our male colleagues?' The naked police officer was now down on her knees where she belonged and patiently awaiting her turn as her partner greedily sucked the manager's cock, desperate both to please him and to swallow an extra large helping of his spunk.

'Yes, that would be lovely,' groaned Mr Johnson with near-orgasmic satisfaction. 'And if you could also make sure that nobody makes any complaints or presses charges against us then I'll be sure to give you both a cup of coffee every day.'

Both women eagerly agreed to the proposition, not caring about little things like corruption as long as they could please their new master. And so having each swallowed so much hot sticky semen that they could still taste it on their lips, the two new puppets got dressed once again and headed back out to their police car, hardly able to wait until they could return the next day. Every problem has a solution and there is no drawback that can't be overcome. And so having dealt with the local constabulary so easily and certain that any straight man who objected could be *persuaded* to change his mind by Jennifer and the rest, Mr Johnson felt absolutely certain that he could deal with any problem that arose.

A few hours later of course, he had the opportunity to prove this theory when, storming through the front door like a righteous bat out of hell, the wife of one of the customers demanded to see the manager. In the time that it took to boil the kettle however, even this problem was solved. And later that night as she fucked her husband like a good little sex toy, Janet pleaded with her husband as only a horny submissive caffeine addict can do.

'Please Michael!' she whimpered pitifully, digging her nails deep into her ankles as the massive cock thrust so deep inside her ass hole that she could feel it in her throat. 'Please can we go back into town tomorrow and buy you another suit! Mr Johnson won't give me another cup of 'coffee unless you buy another suit!'

'But what about the sales girls? You said that you would get really angry if I ever fucked any of them again?'

'I don't mind about that any more! I mean, I had to lick out Angela's pussy before Mr Johnson would let me have another cup and it was really nice! So you can fuck them if you want to! *I'll* fuck them if you want me to! But *please* can we buy you another suit?'

'Okay, darling.' Michael chuckled as he submitted to his wife's heart-warming pleas. He had teased her long enough. 'We'll go buy another suit tomorrow if that's what you really want.' '*Thank you, Master!*' panted the obedient little bitch as Michael prepared to shoot another load of spunk inside her. '*Thank you so…very…MUCH!*'

Fratel
by Adrie Santos

Lisbon was a four-hour train journey away. With each train stop came the possibility of losing the luxury of my private compartment; most likely to a little old man smelling of salami and cheese, or perhaps a caged chicken.

My long blonde hair clung to my sweaty skin and between the straps of my white cami. I concentrated on pulling it free.

The train had just pulled out of Fratel. That was when I heard a voice.

'Desculpe,' apologized the tall, handsome stranger as he put his briefcase down, taking a seat across from me.

'Hello.' I grinned to myself.

He was beautiful; with his olive skin and full black hair, and, surely, the deepest eyes I'd ever seen. He was dressed in dark trousers and a light blue dress shirt – his tie loosened around his open collar; this led me to assume that he was a businessman. I tried not to stare at the sexy creature and could only keep my eyes glued on the window as he was sitting directly in front of me in the small space – so small that our knees were practically touching.

The train moved on, and the vibration of the engine and the intoxicating scent of the passing forests stirred something within me. The heavy feeling in my chest was lifting, and a smile was beginning to form on my face. Was it the enchanting setting or was it the beautiful stranger that was causing all of my senses to waken?

I glanced at him; his head was back, resting against the cushioned wall. His face was a bit flushed; probably from the heat, but hopefully because of me! I wondered what he was thinking of. My eyes wandered over his beautiful face and down his neck, causing me to envision my lips there, softly kissing a path down. He stirred for a second; bringing his hand up to wipe his forehead – boy – it really was getting hot in the compartment! I noticed how large his hands were, and the dark hair that adorned them. I imagined that he would have a perfectly hairy chest, very European – very sexy.

I began to feel a longing building in me and became lost in my fantasy of this handsome foreigner. He and I were in the midst of a passionate kiss when I was startled out of my daydream.

'Muito calor,' he said, fanning himself to imply it was very hot. He went on to roll up his sleeves and remove his tie – all the while looking right into my eyes. His movements were slow and almost looked as if he were performing a little striptease just for me. His deep gaze was enough to make me weak in the knees and hotter than I would have anticipated possible on this ride in the middle of a magical nowhere.

Though a tad dewy from the heat and still a little worn from the tearful goodbye earlier in the day – I knew I was lookin' pretty luscious. I'd intended going out upon my arrival in Lisbon and had paid special attention when dressing that morning – choosing the cami that fitted snugly over my ample bosom and a low-slung denim skirt that had a slit up the centre high enough to offer a glimpse of my panties if I sat just so! And the shoes – my piece de resistance; a pair of white, stiletto-heeled sandals with a tiny strap over the toes and another that wrapped around the back of my ankle and did up in front with a tiny bow! Loved them! And knew that any hot-blooded male would love them too! They were the ideal showcase for my tanned feet and legs.

'Tourista?' he asked while eyeing me up and down.

'Um-hmm.' I smiled back; not letting on that my background was originally the same as his.

My father used to tell me how the men in Europe loved '*touristas*' because they believed that they were easily seduced!

I wasn't about to let on any different – I wanted him to seduce me!

'You are very beautiful,' he whispered, still looking into my eyes.

I responded with a smile, running my fingers slowly along my exposed thigh – matching his intense gaze. My heart felt as if it were dancing around in my chest! I longed for him to kiss me with those full lips and caress me with his strong hands. As we stared brazenly at each other, it became unclear who was seducing whom, but, very clear that we were both ready to act out our intentions.

With one final lick of my lips and toss of my hair, I stood up, never, taking my eyes off of him. I don't know what came over me, but I walked over to the door and pulled down the blind, blocking the view that others passing in the corridor might have into our compartment, and, with that gesture, he too got up and we were standing face to face.

My chest was pressed against his, holding me steady from the motion of the train. He pushed his hands through my hair, holding my face and brought it up to his, pressing his warm lips to mine. His kiss was strong and wet and I felt it through my entire body. I pulled away for a moment and could see he was surprised. He stood, with his lips slightly parted as if about to speak, but no words were needed – I moved in and ran my tongue softly over his bottom lip, at the same time running my hands along his solid body. He reached around and pulled me hard against him and took over my mouth with his, caressing my hair gently.

'Mmmm…Linda' he breathed, barely moving his lips from mine. Hearing him call me beautiful in a foreign tongue made me hotter – it was just so sexy: the language, the accent, the man.

He slid his fingers under the straps of my top and slipped them off my shoulders, following the straps down my arm with soft little kisses. As the tiny little straps slid off, past my hand, he brought my fingers to his mouth, sucking on them one by one. My body trembled as he lowered the cami, revealing my tanned breasts – nipples swollen, ready to be touched. He paused for a moment and just stared in awe; taking in the beauty that I was offering. I began undoing his buttons, but I was not nearly as patient as him; I moved quickly – hungrily and removed his shirt in seconds, quickly forcing my lips to his bare skin and kissing his solid chest before returning to his lips again. His chest felt so good touching mine – my nipples hard against him.

'Eu quero-te…' he said breathlessly as he devoured my

breasts with his mouth, his tongue moving quickly over one nipple and then to the other. He continued to suckle my breast and I held on to him for balance as he pulled on my skirt until it dropped to the floor, then doing the same to the cami until that too lay by my feet. I stood for a moment; hot, wet and almost naked, allowing him to admire me before I undid his pants and pulled them and his boxers down with one movement. When our bodies came together again, I felt consumed by my desire for him – how was it possible to want someone so much? I pushed hard against him, but felt I couldn't get close enough – I needed him inside me. I could feel his hard, swollen cock pressing against my thigh and I wriggled about, trying to bring it to my hungry, waiting slit, but he pulled away, saying softly, 'Let me give you pleasure.'

He guided me down onto the seat.

'Lay back.'

I did so, raising my hips as he removed my panties. Again, his movements were slow and relaxed as he inched the delicate fabric downward, his tongue lightly flicking behind. When they were finally off, I parted my legs for him, making space for him to get in between and do to me as he wished. He placed his hands on my pussy, pulling apart my wet lips. I couldn't help but let out a whimper as he laid his mouth on my swollen clit. My entire body was consumed with shivers of delight as slowly and sensuously he licked and sucked on my cunt.

His tongue moved slowly along every fold, stopping every now and again to take my clit into his lips – it was slow sweet torture. I raised myself off the seat just enough to be able to watch him. His dark hair was slightly ruffled, and his forehead spattered with tiny beads of sweat. His eyes opened slowly, as if he had awakened from some sort

103

of trance. He looked at me and I could see his beautiful eyes smile and feel his desire for me throughout my body. His eyes continued to twinkle, almost mischievously, as he brought two fingers to his own mouth and sucked on them before pushing them slowly into me.

He pumped his fingers in and out of me, curling them up each time, hitting a spot that I had never felt before. His tongue resumed its work on my clit.

All of his movements combined sent quakes of ecstasy through every inch of me. My body felt as if it were on the brink of heaven when he finally got up from in between my legs; his mouth glistening with my juices. He looked into my eyes as he laid himself on top of me. I could feel his damp and swollen cock resting on my thigh.

'I need you.'

His accent sang into my ear as he positioned himself, finally plunging his long cock into my worthy pussy. He seemed to enter me deeper than anyone ever had before and he rested there as if wanting to savour the moment for as long as possible.

I held him there inside me, and we sighed together, both aware that the moment was fleeting. I ran my finger tips down his back until I reached his ass, grabbing hold of his flesh, encouraging him to take me. I had never felt such desperation.

One final sigh and a caress of my face, and he raised his chest up off me. Bracing his arms, he took long, deep thrusts, making sure that I could feel every ridge of his beautiful dick. His lips lingered on my nipples.

Tears of ecstasy rolled down my cheeks as our bodies moved together in unison with the rhythm of the train, each thrust more pleasurable than the last.

He kissed my neck, at the same time whispering sweet

foreign words – pushing me closer and closer to the edge. I tilted my head back – giving myself up to him as my entire body quivered with his touch.

I could see the familiar lights of the Lisbon harbour through the windows above; night had fallen and I knew we were nearing the end of our journey.

One last kiss was all I needed; I pulled his face close and his mouth to mine until our tongues danced together, sending my body into convulsions as I climaxed like never before.

My cries of pleasure drowned out the sound of the train. My insides pulsed and tightened around him as if to hold him and this moment inside me forever. My strong hold of his cock forced him to crisis as well. I could feel him pulsing inside me. He moaned as he came, filling me with his warm milk and finally collapsing on top of me.

We had little time to bask in the afterglow. The train was nearing its final stop.

After dressing quickly and in silence, we kissed goodbye and went our separate ways.

I never dared to look back. The beautiful stranger would remain, in my mind, another lovely memento from my magical trip, one that I would for years relive, each time that I made my journey through the Portuguese countryside – passing Fratel with a smile.

Visiting Time
by Stephen Albrow

Her mini-skirt skimming the tops of her stockings, Lisa strode through the prison gates and took her place at the end of the line.

The guards were goggle-eyed. There were about thirty people queuing up to visit incarcerated love ones that afternoon, but Lisa was different. Everyone else had dressed for the weather, which was overcast and threatening rain, but from her low-cut blouse to her stiletto heels, Lisa had dressed for sex.

The prison doors were opened at two o'clock, the thick metal panels wheeled apart by two burly prison guards. One of them spotted her and gave his colleague a nudge.

'She'll start a bleeding riot,' he muttered.

The breeze played with Lisa's long blonde hair and ruffled the hem of her skirt, giving split-second glimpses of the bare flesh above her stocking tops.

Elevated by her five-inch heels, her long, slim legs seemed to go on forever, the stilettos exaggerating her sexy wiggle.

Feeling the weight of their stare upon her, Lisa turned and winked at the burly guards. She accentuated her wiggle even more, swinging her shapely hips from side to side, as she moved across to the security zone, where a third guard made her raise her arms, then ran an electronic sensor all over her body.

The guard took his time working her over, even dropping to his knees and running his sensor up and down her legs and under her skirt.

Deciding she was a total slut, the other guards shared jokes as they watched. Lisa was happy for them to think whatever they wanted.

'Okay, you can go through now,' said the security guard, still down on his knees looking up Lisa's skirt.

She performed a little curtsey, before returning to her place at the end of the queue.

The registration room was down a long, featureless corridor, which opened out onto a modest lobby. Straight ahead was the door to the visiting room, a tall, muscular guard on either side. To the left was a desk, behind which sat a grey-haired warden, who took each of the visitor's details, after which they were let in to see their miscreant husbands, fathers, sons and lovers.

It was a long, slow wait for Lisa, but she told herself it was worth it. To while away the time, she took out some lip-gloss and a compact mirror from her bag.

Puckering up, she looked to make sure she had the attention of the guards at the door. She did. They were eyeing her up and down – just as she wanted them to.

A trickle of moisture seeped from her pussy.

It was almost her turn to step up to the desk, so the anticipation, both nervous and sexual, began to build up inside her body.

She smiled when the warden finally called her forward. She made a big show of leaning down across his desk, as

108

she picked up the pen and wrote her details in the dog-eared book. The man tried his hardest not to stare down her cleavage-crack, but the low-cut blouse was exposing far too much soft, pink flesh for him to ignore.

The warden looked across at his fellow guards and shook his head from side to side.

Aware of the stir she was creating, Lisa leaned even further across the desk and raised her bottom high into the air. She felt her miniskirt climb high above her black lace stocking tops. The guards at the door were getting a flash of her suspenders, and perhaps even a glimpse of her black silk knickers.

Glancing over her shoulder, she took a quick look at their uniformed crotches. Each had a set of handcuffs and a baton dangling down from their leather belts, but no amount of weaponry could have concealed the swelling pricks beneath.

'I think we might have a problem,' said the elderly warden, slowly rising from his seat.

He motioned for Lisa to wait where she was, then wandered across to talk to his colleagues. The three men formed into a conspiratorial huddle and spoke in whispered voices; their eyes stayed fixed on Lisa.

She could tell her provocative outfit worried the elderly warden. She was being terribly naughty – just as she'd intended. A little more temptation…hitching up her skirt and adjusting a suspender only added further fuel to the flames.

'I'll sort it out,' one of the younger guards said, his voice brimming with bravado, then he walked across to Lisa, who was still toying with her stocking tops.

She met his boyish grin with a seductive, impish smile. He didn't budge but waited for her to let her skirt fall back in place, then asked if she would follow him.

'Sure,' said Lisa, happy to follow the strong, handsome guard almost anywhere.

As she followed, she studied him. He looked exactly what she was looking for, over six foot tall, with big, broad shoulders, his upper body tapering down in a V-shape towards his muscular buttocks.

His navy-blue uniform was freshly washed and ironed, giving him a crisp, clean appearance that was matched by his smoothly-shaven face. His handcuffs jangled as he walked. The only other noise echoing off the grim walls were Lisa's dagger-like heels noisily click-clacking upon the concrete floor.

They were walking along a featureless corridor. At the end of it they entered a small, dark room, only one step up from a prison cell.

'There's a problem with your outfit,' announced the dark-haired guard, shutting the door and locking it.

She gazed around the threadbare room, which contained just a table, a chair and a large metal cabinet. A tiny barred window let in a few shafts of daylight, but otherwise all was cold and dank.

'My outfit?'

Lisa perched on the table and crossed one leg over the other.

She didn't have to look down to know her patterned stocking tops were back on display. The guard's puppy dog eyes were hypnotized by her long, slim legs.

It didn't last. He had a job to do and he was going to do it!

'Your outfit,' said the guard, walking over to the grey metal cabinet and pulling open the doors. Dangling from hangers were a number of prison warden's regulation overcoats. He picked one out and turned back to Lisa. 'You have to cover yourself.'

'I hope you're not expecting me to put that on,' she said, pouting, Lolita-like, at the hunky guard. 'Don't you like the way I'm dressed?' she teased, her eyes fixed upon the bulge in his trousers. There was no need for him to answer her question, since the ten-inch tent he'd pitched in his pants made it all too clear just how much he loved her slutty attire.

'It's not about what I like,' argued the guard, trying to remain professional. 'There are guys in this prison that haven't had sex with a woman for over twenty years. If they see you in that skirt and top, then God only knows what will happen in there!'

'Oops,' said Lisa, giggling at the thought, as she jumped down from the table. 'Have I been a bad girl?' she asked the guard, stepping right up to his well-built body, before turning round and bending over.

'It's not a question of being a bad girl,' said the guard, trying not to look at her behind. Her skirt had risen high above her waist, revealing the womanly contours of her perfect arse, her tight black knickers cutting into each cheek.

'Oh, please say I'm a bad girl,' Lisa begged, stepping forward and leaning across the table, butt exposed to his gaze.

She parted her thighs, allowing the musky scent of the moisture on her knickers to perfume the room.

Closing his eyes, the guard breathed in the tempting, intoxicating odour. This was above and beyond the call of duty. He was used to dealing with hardened criminals, so strange behaviour was nothing new to him. But nothing in his training had prepared him for this.

'Just put on the coat and you can make your visit,' said the guard, opening his eyes and holding out the overcoat.

'No,' said Lisa.

'Do as I say,' the guard insisted, with greater assertiveness in his voice. He was beginning to get angry now, so when Lisa refused to obey again, something inside him seemed to snap.

'Okay, if that's the way you want it,' he yelled.

Just as she'd hoped, he whipped his handcuffs off his belt, walked around the table and then drew up the chair. He fixed a handcuff to one of Lisa's wrists, looped the chain through the slats in the back of the chair, then handcuffed her other wrist, rendering her immobile.

'Happy now?' he asked.

Lisa tugged at the chair but couldn't break free. Lying flat across the table, with her arse poking up in the air, she was completely at the warden's mercy. Widening her baby blue eyes, she stared over her shoulder at his handsome face, an impudent smirk upon her lips. Catching his smouldering gaze, she nodded towards the baton dangling down from his belt. Unsmiling, the warden reached for the nine-inch rubber crop, then stepped up behind his female captive.

'You're nothing but a slut,' he said, raising the baton shoulder-high and preparing to strike. It fizzed through the air and slapped against her knickers.

She moaned, but refused to give in.

Unconcerned by her discomfort, he followed straight up with a shorter, firmer strike trained on the back of her thighs.

Her groan was even louder second time around. This time he'd hit an area of bare flesh, not one cushioned by the soft and silky knickers.

Seemingly pleased and wanting more bare flesh to aim at, the guard tugged her knickers right down, then once more raised his baton high.

'You're a bad girl,' he grunted, delivering a fearful spank to Lisa's curvaceous arse.

Her whole body spasmed, recoiling from the burst of pain, but still she pushed out her buttocks further, as if demanding another firm lash.

Calling her a dirty bitch, the guard set out to fulfil her wishes, executing a blow so fierce it left a bright red mark on Lisa's buttocks. The captive responded with a howl of pain. She pulled at the handcuffs, like she wanted to break free, but the guard could tell the opposite was true – Lisa loved every minute of her subjugation.

'Call me a bitch again,' she begged him, wiggling her buttocks enticingly.

'Okay, you're a bitch!'

Another blow landed, this time aimed at the sore spot for maximum impact.

The thick prison walls absorbed the tortured shriek that burst from Lisa's gaping mouth; then her breath grew heavy, as her insides started pulsing.

All of a sudden, the lips of her pussy were twitching in anticipation of the prison guard's cock; more and more juice was seeping out of her slit, its luscious scent inflaming the desire of the dark, dominant man.

'How wet are you, bitch,' he said, digging his baton between Lisa's legs.

The rubber truncheon brushed through her sticky cunt lips, poking against her clitoris and making her moan.

The prison guard unzipped his trousers and let them fall around his ankles. Withdrawing the rubber baton, he shoved in his own, which was just as hard.

He spanked her buttocks while feeding in over half of his ten-inch prick, pulling back, and then once again pumping the entire length inside.

Lisa's cunt began to convulse around his rock-hard shaft, but the guard was easily strong enough to fuck his way through the lustful spasms. Gripping one of her thighs with one hand and wielding the baton with the other, he powered his cock in and out of her pussy.

'Take that, you slut!'

He continued to spank her with the baton as he fucked her. Her squealing excited him. His rock-hard dick plunged deeply between her tensed up cunt muscles. The squeal of pain turned into a long, deep groan of intense satisfaction.

He withdrew to the entrance of her pussy, then split her cunt down the middle all over again. As her moans grew even louder, he leaned forward and stuffed the baton between her lips, gagging her with the punishment tool.

Lisa bit into the rubber baton and tasted her own pussy.

As she flicked her tongue at the sticky surface, the guard slid his hands towards her stocking tops. He fucked her slowly. He fucked her quickly. He fucked until she felt she could die with pleasure.

The lower tempo of the thrusts seemed to heighten the sensitivity for both of them, but Lisa wasn't interested in sensitivity that day – quite the opposite, she wanted her pussy to take the same kind of pounding that her buttocks had only just received.

Wanting to be fucked hard again, wanting to be fucked like a bad girl, Lisa began to grind her hips along with the prison guard's thrusts. Their bodies rocked as one, but it was her applying most of the pressure that forced the prison guard back into a high-speed tempo.

Gripping her hips, he hammered his lengthy cock in and out of her cunt, each thrust delivered with more venom than the last.

Lisa closed her eyes. The guard's long, thick cock was thumping in and out of her slick, wet orifice, sparkling tingles of pleasure throughout her cunt. She felt the thick, metal handcuffs chafe the outer layer of skin off her wrists, as the force of the fuck made everything shake. She could feel her rigid nipples digging into the wooden surface; her full breasts now squashed almost flat. Her teats were tingling with almost the same intensity as her cock-filled pussy, so when the guard reached for the sensitive buds, her whole body erupted with climactic delight.

He tightened his fingers around her teats, squeezing them till they almost burst. His cockhead had already started throbbing, but the pulsations in his head increased tenfold, as the climactic contractions shooting through Lisa's pussy made her muscles close in around his prick. Juices were flooding out of her orifice, making her cunt even wetter and much more pliable. Taking advantage of the added pliability, the guard geared up for a final thrust.

The first jet of spunk spurted out of his prick. He threw his head back, eyes closed, sounds of ecstasy pouring from his throat. One more quick thrust delivered more spunk out of his bulging head.

Lisa's pussy responded with a sequence of fierce contractions, as if her cunt and the prison guard's helmet were trying to outdo each other with the force of their orgasmic throbs. She felt confident of winning the battle, since her climactic rush showed no signs of fading. The gag in her mouth was restraining her, bottling up the sexual tension, rather than allowing her a full release.

The guard heard her mumbling. The baton was still in her mouth. Finally, she let it go.

'Spank me one more time,' she said like the slut she was.

Calling her a dirty slut, he landed more blows with the baton across her buttocks, only this time she was free to yell.

Dropping to his knees, the prison guard pressed his face between her thighs, licking up the juices that came pouring out of her cunt.

She felt his warm, wet tongue sliding all over her orifice, stimulating her already buzzing clit until she simply couldn't take anymore.

Suddenly craving kisses, she begged the hunky guard to set her free, so he walked round the table and undid the heavy handcuffs. Instantly, their bodies came together in a passionate embrace, the blistering heat of their recent orgasms fuelling the intense desire in their deep-throat kisses.

Lost in post-orgasmic ecstasy, the prison guard finally came to his senses.

He took a long, hard look into Lisa's eyes, as if slowly coming round from a dream.

'You better get your clothes back on,' the prison guard said, trying to regain some sense of professionalism. He zipped up his trousers and re-attached his handcuffs to his belt. 'You better put the overcoat on, as well so you can go and visit whoever it is you came to see.'

Giggling, Lisa bent down to pick up her knickers, a knowing smile spread across her face.

'Who did you come to visit?' the prison guard asked, suddenly keen to know which of the villainous inmates was the husband or lover of this curious girl.

'Oh, no one in particular,' Lisa said. 'Just anyone with a handsome face, a pair of handcuffs and a rubber baton.'

Matter-of-factly, she straightened out her hair, then tucked her breasts back into her blouse. 'I mean, why else do you think I dressed like this? I knew I was certain of being noticed by someone like you.'

The prison guard's eyebrows furrowed even further, as the implications of what she said dawned on him. He watched her as she continued to readjust her clothing, no longer quite so certain that it had been him who'd been calling the shots.

'I like being treated like a bad girl,' Lisa added with a wide smile 'so what better place to come to than a prison?'

The guard shrugged his shoulders, then opened the door. Visiting time was officially over. It was time to release his prisoner back into the world.

Two's Company
by Georgina Brown

The bedroom door was ajar. Soft, creamy satin covered the bed. The pillows were also of satin.

The last rays of sunset picked out her head on the pillow, her hair a bluish-black against the creamy shine of satin.

On the other pillow he saw blonde hair. At first he caught his breath and felt a huge surge of anger. She had been unfaithful to him, she who had promised not to sleep with any other man unless he was present. This one had his arm around her and was vaguely familiar.

In a sudden rush of recognition, he knew it was no man lying there, but her best friend, Gloria. Both girls were asleep and doubtless naked. But to him it didn't really matter if two girls had been playing at being lovers. Una had not betrayed him.

Spellbound and clad only in his trousers now, he stared at the two beautiful women, their creamy arms thrown across each other.

Suddenly, he was smitten with the enchantment of the scene. His heart became full of love, his body full of desire.

There could be no course of action open to him except the one he had in mind. Imagine, he thought. Man's greatest desire, to be in bed between two women. The thought made him shiver. He asked himself whether they were likely to protest. He couldn't know for sure.

Test the water.

It was all he could do.

Silently, he stepped out of his trousers and what remained of his clothes.

Penis standing proud and ready, he stepped forward and got onto the bed. They murmured something as he began to edge between them, snuggling down under their entwined limbs. As he did so, he sighed loud and long and closed his eyes. If it was good to go to sleep with a woman's body up against his, it was even better when it was two women in the bed.

'What?' Una said it slowly, blearily, and opened her eyes. 'Ben! What are you doing here?'

He smiled in what he considered a disarming way. 'I wanted to see you.'

He had wanted to say 'fuck you', but decided on the softly, softly approach. Mr Romance, here I come!

His strategy obviously worked. Her body came closer, pressed against his. Her arms encircled him and her lips were on his, on his neck, on his chest.

Gloria, Una's friend, stirred behind him, her strong perfume drifting over his shoulder.

He felt the thick bush of her pubic hair against his buttocks, felt her lips on his shoulders.

'Honey,' he heard her say in a sleepy voice.

Gloria did not usually do anything for his libido, but this was an exceptional circumstance. He murmured with pleasure as the warmth of their bodies pressed more positively against his. By his presence alone, he had ignited some unseen fire in them. Their torsos undulated against him like waves against a beach.

'Keep doing that,' he murmured. 'Keep doing that for ever.'

Their hands seemed to be all over him at once. He felt he was drifting away on a tide of sheer decadence. Pleasure had become a magic carpet ride.

One female hand cupped his balls, while another pulled on his stem. Their other hands caressed his chest, his belly, and their lips landed like butterflies on his mouth, his neck and his chest.

They were pulling on him, urging his member to dance with the advance of rising semen. He was at no pains to stop them. His throat was dry, his voice trapped in his throat.

He was still lying on his side when Gloria's free hand began to caress his behind. As she did this, Una raised her leg, bent her knee and rested it over his leg. Her pussy came closer. Her sexual lips opened, and her mouth clamped swiftly over his.

Springing like a creature from cover, his prick leapt forward, its head nudging into the fleshy crack between her thighs.

It was so easy, so delicious to slide into her. With a thrust of his pelvis, half his weapon gained entry. With a second thrust, his whole length filled her body. His pubic hair rasped against hers.

All the while, Gloria's hand caressed his behind and crept into the gap between his legs to play with his balls.

The sensations from this were incredible. Gloria was manipulating his balls, not just for his benefit or her own, but also for that of Una. As Gloria's caresses became more positive, his whole body seemed to surge into Una, his penis swelling under pressure from what was happening within and without.

Every vein in his neck felt as if it were bursting. Every fibre of his being was helpless in their hands.

Just when he felt he had reached the zenith of their ministrations, Gloria's finger ran down between his cheeks and jabbed fiercely at the aperture between. He cried out, his back arching, his pelvis thudding against that of Una.

It was as if he had been speared; as if he was no more than a monkey on a stick dancing to someone else's tune.

His essence spurted out of him. Even if he had wanted to hold it back, to play for time until Una had reached her orgasm, he could not have done so.

Whatever these women wanted they would take. And whatever they wanted, he would give it to them.

Una kissed him once he was fully spent. Her fingers ran through his hair, slid down over his ear. She traced circles around its outer edge.

He looked into her eyes. Even in the semi-darkness of the room, they still sparkled. Again he felt helpless.

'Have we finished with him yet?' Una said to Gloria.

Gloria giggled behind him. Her finger was still embedded in his anus. He tried to wriggle off.

'Not so fast,' Gloria said against his ear. 'Didn't you hear what Una said? We haven't finished with you yet.'

'Greedy girls,' he said. 'What do you want now?'

Their bodies became like clothes that fitted a little too tightly.

'We're going to give you exactly what you deserve.'

They stretched his arms over his head and tied his wrists to the towering posts of the cast iron bed.

A sudden worry crossed his mind. 'Is this going to

hurt?'

'Not much.' It was Gloria who answered.

He began to struggle.

Una laid her hands on his chest. Her lovely face came close to his.

'Don't worry, darling. Lie back and enjoy it, there's a good boy. If you don't, Una will smack your naughty bottom or stick things into it that it just won't like!'

Gloria got out of bed and went to the bathroom. He could hear her using the lavatory.

When she came back, she held a long, orange-coloured bottle in one hand.

'What's that?' he asked as she took out the stopper.

'Oil,' murmured Una as she flicked her fingers at his hair and kissed his brow. 'Don't look so worried. It really is only oil.'

His lips suddenly felt incredibly dry. He ran his tongue over them. They did not improve.

Gloria's fingers fastened around his limp weapon.

He groaned. 'Oh, no! Not again!'

The girls cuddled up to him.

'But darling, you've had what you came for. Now what about us?' Una exclaimed.

'That's right, darling,' added Gloria. 'You might think it's just fun going to bed with two women, but every pleasure has to be paid for. Two women are hard work – as you, my darling, are about to find out!'

To his great surprise, his stiffness returned. Una and Gloria stroked his purple-veined protrusion which was already delivering a spit of salt-laden juice from its throbbing head.

Despite his fear of not being able to perform – because fear was really what it was all about – he found himself murmuring with pleasure. Their hands were all over him, stroking his chest, his belly, nibbling at his ears, his neck and his throat.

Una's mouth covered his and suppressed the groan that accompanied Gloria's nibbling of his balls. He could feel her soft cheeks against his inner thighs, her nose against his stem.

Strong and newly virile, his penis stood up. Chest heaving, he watched as Una got astride his pelvis and lowered herself onto his phallus. Slowly but surely, the whole length was gobbled up by her body.

Beyond her he could se Gloria bent between his thighs, her bottom high in the air, her teeth still nibbling at his balls as Una rode his stem.

The urge to catch up with her and fill her with his semen was extremely powerful, but he was not given the chance.

'My turn!' he heard Gloria cry.

They swapped places.

Ben knew he was being used, but could do nothing to stop it – not that he wanted to.

The lips of Gloria's plump pussy slid down over his length.

He groaned with pleasure as Una lifted his leg and began licking from his scrotum and into his crack.

'Give me more,' he heard Gloria say.

He tried to protest. 'Girls, I can't take much more.'

They ignored him and spoke to each other.

'Is he letting you down?' Una asked Gloria.

'This stud is not doing his best,' Gloria responded.

Una sighed. 'Oh dear. Then I'll have to deal with it. Now let's see if I can find his 'g' spot again.'

Ben cried out and arched his back as Una's finger

pushed into his anus. She did not ease it in, testing to see if it pained or pleasured him. She pushed it straight in up to the hilt so that his hips rose from the bed and his penis rammed home more fiercely into Gloria's accommodating vagina.

Because the response was so fierce, he could not stop the vessel that ran the length of his penis from filling up with fluid. Neither could he stop it from racing to the tip of his shaft and spilling like foaming milk into the waiting Gloria.

He groaned when Una said she wanted him to fuck her too.

'Oh come on, Ben. Isn't this what threesomes are all about? Everyone getting what they want?'

Still tied to the bed, he did as she required as best he could, though the sight of her ass and his penis disappearing between her cheeks did go some way to help.

Hours later – though it seemed longer to him – they finally untied him.

'We'll rest for now, and try again later.'

That was their plan, but it wasn't his. Once they were asleep, he eased himself out from in between them, ostensibly to go to the bathroom.

His clothes were where he'd left them. The girls were still sleeping. He was out of there.

'Two's company, three's a...' The usual phrase was that three was a crowd. In his threesome fantasy it was the girls who did the work.

On weary legs, his penis sleeping like a squashed giblet in his pants, he exited stage left.

Threesomes, he decided, were a bloody nightmare!

The First Time
by J. Johnson

'This is for you,' her father said.

The bicycle was old and might once have been plain black. Now it was painted bright blue and was plenty good enough to cycle around the flat roads that radiated out from the railway line that ran all the way to Marseilles.

The day she met Paul, battalions of poplars threw straight shadows across the road and the sun was polishing the sky bright blue.

Wearing only knickers, sandals and a blue dress that was too short to cover her long, brown legs and too tight across her developing bosom, she pushed off along the flat stretch that ran from the farmhouse towards the village and the river.

Riding over the alternate stripes of sunlight and shade dappling the road was hypnotic but also, after a while, somehow disturbing Eventually she took a left along a clay-baked path that led through a field to the orchard beyond.

The grass beneath the apple trees was long and scattered all over with pink petals fallen from the trees. The ground was uneven; mounds of earth thrown skywards by burrowing moles pock-marked the grassy spaces. Without braking properly, she let the front wheel hit the first hillock. The bike tumbled in one direction while she tumbled in the other. She collapsed in the cool grass, arms above her head, eyes closed and breasts heaving.

A light breeze blew the last of the blossom over her to lie like confetti in her hair and down her body. She sighed with satisfaction and stretched her limbs.

Don't open your eyes. Just lie here and enjoy it. And unbutton your dress, she added. It's too childish and too small. Your bosoms might get stunted even before they're fully-grown – and you want full bosoms. Didn't every girl?

Still with her eyes closed, she unbuttoned her dress and pushed the tight fitting bodice to the sides so her nipples looked at the sky and the breeze and the blossom fluttered over her firm flesh.

Lovely!

She groaned and arched her back. It was as if the breeze had fingers, perhaps even a mouth. She smiled to herself and wondered what it would feel like if it were a real man running his fingers lightly over her body, and taking a nipple between his lips.

She could only pretend.

'This is a man,' she whispered. Keeping her eyes tightly closed she ran her hands over her fledgling breasts and felt her nipples hardening beneath her touch.

This is a man's fingers, she told herself as she traced delicate circles around her nipples before pinching them and marvelling at how quickly they became hard. She also noticed a light tingling between her legs.

'If only...' she murmured running one hand down over

her belly. She sighed and would have drifted off to sleep if it hadn't suddenly seemed cooler.

Just a cloud passing over the sun, she thought.

'Mademoiselle?'

Not a cloud!

She sat bolt upright. A young man stood between her and the summer sun. His shadow fell over her.

'What do you want?' she blurted, hurriedly covering her bosoms with her hands, her skirt still crumpled over the top of her thighs.

'Can you spare some water?' he asked, looking at her a little quizzically.

'Of course.' She nodded at the plastic bottle clipped to the handlebars. 'Please. Take some.'

All the while as he tipped the water down into his throat he watched her over the top of the bottle and she held his gaze. Inexperienced as she was, she understood the look in his eyes and that he was studying her barely concealed breasts, her brown legs.

Her hands began to fall away. His eyes, even the way his throat moved as he drank, excited her. In turn she looked at him.

Golden hairs shone on his bare brown legs and arms. He wore only a t-shirt and cut off jeans.

Once he'd finished drinking, he pulled his t-shirt over his head and wiped his face with it.

Deanna stared at his body. Her eyes stayed fixed on the firm flesh until she became aware that he was offering the water bottle back to her. She took it and gulped down mouthfuls, surprised that she was suddenly so thirsty.

'That's better,' she said with a sigh of satisfaction. 'I feel cooler now.'

'I dare say you do,' he said, smiling appreciatively and

nodding at her bare breasts.

'I needed to cool down after cycling,' she said. 'And to cool down you must expose as much surface area as possible,' she added with a provocative shrug of her shoulders which exposed even more flesh than before.

One eyebrow rose and he smiled in a crooked kind of way that betrayed what he was thinking. 'I know what you mean.' He flexed his biceps and laughed.

She laughed with him.

Without invitation he flopped on the grass beside her, bent his arm and supported his head in his hand. 'I think you are what they call a bit of a madam,' he said.

She tossed her hair and lay back in the grass and stared up at the trees and sky overhead. Although the smell of apple blossom was still strong, it was overwhelmed by the scent of his body, a smell she had not got this close to before, not like this.

He reached out and touched her breast. Her excitement intensified. His fingers traced lines around her nipples. He bent his head and gently kissed each adolescent orb.

If this was wrong, she didn't care. Sweet, physical urges that had only recently come into being were surging upwards, making her flesh tingle and causing her stomach muscles to tighten until she thought she would burst.

A sudden anguish caught hold of her as she felt her white cotton knickers being pulled over her feet. If only they weren't so girlish. If only she had known she would meet him today, she would have borrowed a pair belonging to Maeve, her father's mistress. They were usually made of satin.

The grass was especially cool against her bottom. In a strange way she wanted to look down at her belly and thighs, to see with him the clutch of dark hair nestling

130

there. She wanted to see what he was seeing, know what he was thinking.

Perhaps it wasn't done to look. She wouldn't know. This would be the first time. She must forget that he was here; she wanted to fully appreciate every kiss, every touch.

'Won't you look at me?' he said as he lay outstretched on her body.

'It's enough to feel you.' She was speaking the truth. His body was hard against hers. His breath was warm on her face and the smell of him, a mix of fresh sweat and youthful hormones, was absolutely intoxicating.

His fingers explored between her legs. Something screamed, 'that's it!' in her body. One little place! That especially! She gasped and mewed for more. What was that thing? It seemed such a small area, no bigger than a button yet at the touch of his finger its sensitivity seemed to spread all over her body.

'I like that,' she said and threw her arms around his neck. He kissed her on the mouth, his lips warm and demanding, his tongue diving in on top of hers, just as his body was on top of hers.

'I think,' he said, his voice thick with lust as he grappled with his zip, 'that you'll like this even better.'

Hard and warm, he guided it to where it should be.

Merely the tip at first, nudging aside her pubic lips, tapping gently yet deliberately at that tiny button of powerful sensitivity.

Warm, she thought, like velvet.

Her stomach muscles tightened. She knew what was to come next. Was she ready?

It's going, she thought as the first inches of stiff penis entered her. My virginity is going! This is my special moment. This is my first time and I should feel pain, but instead I feel only pleasure.

Her outer flesh parted to let him in. Her inner flesh encompassed the male member, curving around it, gripping it as he rocked backwards and forwards, backwards and forwards.

Something intensified, something gathered pressure, built up and up and...

It exploded!

A wave of pleasure swept over her and made her feel she no longer had form, only sensation, sexuality, and a feeling that she had stepped into the next chapter of her life.

The young man with the blond hair thrust one more time, tensed above her then flopped onto the grass.

She didn't look at him but closed her eyes and savoured the moment. He wanted her to say something. She knew that. He wanted her to say how wonderful he was and to swoon like any other silly young girl. But she wasn't any other girl.

Her silence finally got to him. 'What are you thinking?' he asked.

She heard the neediness in his voice. He wanted flattery, but that wasn't what was in her mind.

'I'm committing this moment to memory. This was my first time. When I'm old and grey I want to remember this moment, to relive it and recall how I feel now.'

His shadow fell over her as he got up and dressed. He looked aggrieved.

'Will I see you again?' he asked.

She smiled. 'Sometimes. Possibly in your dreams.'

So Come See Me, OK?
by Thomas Fuchs

Look at me, want me, reach for me. Reach up here for me, baby. Yeah, it's you I'm dancing for. Give yourself a thrill, baby, slip a bill in my thong and let your hand slide over my bulge.

When the coloured strobes are flashing I'm mysterious, exotic and hot, hot, hot, and when the steady lights come on, I still look real good, right? Even better, huh?

Like my muscles, baby? So big and smooth. Flex my arms for you. Turn around for you, grind my ass.

Look at those big, round cheeks doing their own little dance for you, up and down, side to side, back and forth, in and out, huh, yeah! And turn again and thrust. Look at these abs, baby, cut deep, huh? And my chest, my pecs, swelling mountains of muscle. You want to bury your face in them, lick these nipples, suck 'em, make me hard for you baby, huh? See how my dick's swelling against my jock, hot for you, yeah, hot for you.

How did I get to be such a hot number? You think it's just the gym, and swimming, and other sports when I was a kid, and diet and some supplements? Yeah, there's all that physical stuff, but believe me that's all nothing if you haven't got attitude. You gotta have attitude and I do and this is the story of how I got it.

Okay, well, you know I'm pretty well built but here are my stats – 5'10", 180lbs, 46 chest, 29 waist, 16 ½ arms and so forth. Black hair, brown eyes. Smooth skin, good tan, no tan line. Cut, a good eight inches, really, with a nice kind of mushroomy head.

The thing is though, that even with these stats, you might be surprised to hear that I didn't always think I was that much of a stud.

You know how it is, don't you? You look in the mirror and see that you don't really have the cut, or your ab def could be deeper. There's this guy you've seen at the gym or on the street or in one of the mags who's got this or that, so you work harder and harder. Sometimes when I went into the bars, I'd watch the go-go boys and thought wow! I guess some part of me wanted to be up there, but I didn't dare try for it.

Of course, sometimes when I went out, guys would look at me but nobody talked to me. You know, there's a lot of attitude in West Hollywood. Well, some guys sometimes tried to say hi, but not my type, I have to say. And I was too shy to say anything to the guys I wanted to talk to. I was pretty new to all this, from Nevada. Elko, Nevada, which doesn't have anything like the WeHo scene, which of course is why I came here.

I got a job in a Kinko's and another guy there, when we had lunch one day, told me he thought I was really hot but he said I didn't know how to dress. He was a great guy, I have to say, a sister if you know what I mean, trying to help a poor country boy.

He told me I should dress hotter. 'Those shirts from Sears have got to go,' he said. I didn't really get my shirts from Sears but I sort of knew what he meant, so my next day off, I went shopping, in those glitz stores on Santa Monica Boulevard, you know?

And that's when it happened. I was looking at muscle shirts, sleeveless shirts, low-cut tank tops, trying to get up my nerve about which to buy and I tried one on and this guy came over and told me I looked good in the shirt but I could do even better. He was young and pretty hot, with a blond buzz cut and what I guess you would call hazel eyes. He was really nice to me, but that was just because he was a salesman there. That's what I thought, anyway. I never did find out his name, come to think of it.

He said that I should be careful not to get anything that was too obvious because that would be a little slutty and I was classy. He picked out a few shirts for me but when I started into the changing room, he pulled me toward a little stairway and said, 'Come on upstairs. There's more privacy there.'

There wasn't a changing room up there, just a little office, with a desk, a chair, and a couch. When I asked him if it was okay for us to be there, he said, 'Yeah, it's okay. I'm the owner.'

I put on the first shirt he'd picked out for me. Kind of violet or purple and it did show off my skin pretty nicely. Sleeveless, to show my arms and tight enough so you can see some of my chest cut. He was right. I did look pretty good in it.

I was still looking in the mirror when he came up behind me and said, 'You've got it, man. You've got it,' and while I was still figuring out what that meant exactly, he reached around and put his hand on my chest and said, 'Man, you are built, aren't you?'

I knew what that meant of course.

Then he slid his hand down to my dick.

I pulled away a little, you know automatically, 'cos I was a little surprised but even as I did, at the same time, I popped a big and hard one right then and there.

So we stood apart for a second and he said, 'A shy one, are you?'

'No.'

He took my arm, pulled me over to the couch and pushed me down. He put his hand on my dick, more gently now. 'Man,' he said, 'you're like iron there.' He pulled off my pants, and you could really see my dick pushing out against my briefs.

'You must not be comfortable, all cooped up in there,' he said.

He was, you know, pretending like he was talking to my dick. Then he pulled my briefs off and sure enough, my boner slapped up and flat against my stomach.

I thought he'd go right down on me but instead he leaned over and got his tongue on one of my nipples and started licking. I could feel it go hard right away, and he sucked and it felt so good and he was rubbing the other one as he sucked and then he switched, sucking the other nip and rubbing the first one. Made me tingle all over, like some kind of electricity or something was running through me and I think I was making this moaning sound, and all of a sudden it was too much so I got my hand in his hair and pulled him away.

I thought he was going to take a break but he dove down onto my neck this time and his tongue was like flicking on my throat. That was a little yucky so I asked him to stop, and he switched to my ear and the funny thing is that even though I didn't completely like what he was doing, I was thrashing all over and my dick was big and stiff and it was whipping around and I could feel the ooze starting to come out of it.

Then he stopped working my ears and rose up above me, looking down on me and he got this really big grin on his face. He had beautiful lips and when he smiled like that, I knew something nice and juicy was coming.

When he went down on me, he took it in all the way, so the head of my dick was at the back of his mouth even a little down his throat and he swallowed against it and that hot wet pressure felt S..O..O..O…good.

He squeezed and relaxed and squeezed and relaxed and I would'a shot down his throat right then except that at the same time he was pumping me with his throat he had his lips clamped tight around the middle of my cock so the come couldn't come up.

Then he drew his mouth back along the shaft, with his tongue working the whole way and he licked the top of my dick and then back down. He did this a couple of times and then he stopped and grinned at me again, that big something's-coming grin except he didn't dive in on me again. He got off me, off the couch, onto the floor, on his knees, with his smooth white butt stuck up high in the sky.

Well, I sure wanted to work him, but I wasn't really all that experienced at fucking at that time, to tell you the truth, so I studied that hole of his. Seemed nice and clean so I poked my dick onto it, and he said, 'Hey, man, use a rubber, ok?' He reached under the couch, pulled out a little box, got lube and condoms and handed them to me.

I got the rubber on and lubed and started to push.

'Ow, ow,' he said.

He was pretty tight.

'Massage it a little, okay?' he said. 'Use your fingers.'

So I did, around his hole, and it opened up and I slipped

137

my finger in and slid it back and forth and round and he said, 'Ah, ah,'…liking that a lot.

Then he told me to push in two fingers and find the prostate, that hard little thing in there which of course I'd heard about but wasn't too sure about. I was still pretty new to this, you know, but I found it and he told me move my fingers real fast back and forth, and I did and he started moaning and all and grabbing his dick.

And suddenly my dick was like, it felt like it was gonna explode, so I pulled out my fingers and slid my dick in and it's pretty big around so I had to push it and he opened up more but still stayed tight.

It felt so good to be inside him. I went in slow, past the prostate and up. I think I was slamming into his guts and he's going 'Ugh, oofff' and sounds like that. So I asked him if he was okay and he said yeah, man, and he did the most amazing thing. He bent back, turned his head and I leaned forward, really shoving my dick in, and then we kissed.

He pushed his tongue into my mouth, slow and deep a couple of times and then a few real quick, you know like a lizard. Have you ever watched a lizard's tongue shooting in and out? It was like that. Got me even more worked up. Then he pulled his mouth away and said, 'Like that, big fella, fuck me like that.' Then he stuck his tongue back in and did it all again, the slow and deep and then fast and shallow and then deep again. Then he stopped and said, 'Get a rhythm going and then vary it. Like you're dancing. Fuck me like you're dancing, okay?'

So that's what I did. Remember, my dick was in him all through this kissing so now I pushed in slow and deep and when I pulled back slow it was like a pump, like I was sucking his guts. He was making great noises and saying stuff like man oh man and I slow pumped him a couple of times and then speeded up, fast and shallow, and then slow again. And grinding my hips and all kinds of switching around from fast to slow and back again.

Suddenly right in the middle of all this, I flashed on those go-go boys and I had a rhythm going, really going and I was just fucking the daylights out of this guy.

He was holding his dick through all this and now he says 'I'm gonna come, I gotta…' and he shot, great big loads of hot white stuff and that was because of me, what I did to him!

I pulled out, and pulled off the rubber and jumped up. I was stroking myself and dancing! Yes! Dancing, moving my body like I never moved it before and then finally I let go and man it flew through the air, flew, a great big load and another and another and I fell down, just exhausted and at the same time more full of life than I ever remember ever feeling before.

So really, that was how I learned to dance the way I do on the platform. So here I am, so come on in some night. I want you, I need you there, baby. Yeah, I do it for the money but you know what, mostly I do it to see the look on your face, on all your faces, when I'm up here. You're my mirror, kind of. When I look at you looking at me, I know I'm hot.

So come on in, okay? I'm always trying new routines and I'm still growing and getting bigger and hotter. I'm still young. Did I mention that I'm 19? Can you stand it?

Anthony
by Gwen Masters

I decided later it had to be that way he looked at me over dinner; the way he wore that jacket as if it were tailored for him. The way his low voice dropped even lower when he was getting aroused and trying not to show it. Or maybe it was the way he drove that Lexus, the way he rested his wrist over the wheel as if so sure of himself.

No. No, it had to be the way he kissed, so uncertain and shy. That was it. The way he kissed. That is what put me over the edge of reason and into the realm of rhyme.

That's why I went to bed with him.

His body was long and lean, surprisingly muscular. His voice was a deep rasp that got even deeper when he was excited. His hands shook on mine as he moved above me. Slow and gentle, not quite inside me yet, teasing me with the thrill of his hardness against my thighs. Just enough to make the anticipation stretch all over me like a covering of lust mixed with sweat.

His long blond hair fell over me, slipping into my mouth, tickling my ears. I sucked on a strand of it. It tasted clean and pure. His lips tasted like salt and his tongue tasted like limes.

'Jesus Christ, girl. I want you more than you know.'

'Sure feels like it.'

He smiled in the dim light of the candles. I felt it against my throat. I tried to move my hands away from his, to touch him in all the ways I craved, but it felt like steel bands restrained me. He held me effortlessly.

Dear Lord, but he's strong, I thought.

Then I thought nothing else, because he slipped his cock inside me.

I was wetter than I had ever been, and was instantly filled with him. The shock of it made me gasp. My cries were caught in his mouth as if he could taste my very breath. The muscles in his arms tensed and relaxed with the same rhythm of his hips.

'Oh, God,' I cried.

He buried his face in my shoulder and moved faster. The warmth began to spread outward from my pussy, telling me I was close, telling us both. He whispered into my ear.

'You like that, don't you? You should see your face. You haven't had a good fuck in a long time, have you?' There was a pause as he let go of one of my hands. He caught a handful of hair and I moaned with anticipation even before I felt the harsh pull. My head tilted back.

'Answer me,' he demanded.

'What?' I was practically incoherent.

'How long has it been since you had a cock fuck you as hard as you could stand?'

'God…uh…months…'

'Good.'

He went at me in a hard thrust. I screamed at the top of my lungs. To hell with the neighbours.

'Good girl,' he growled.

142

My pussy clenched down on him and made him shiver. I felt it run through him as I ran my hand through his hair and pulled his head back. I licked his throat and savoured the feeling of being satisfied. For the time being. He pumped harder.

'You can fuck harder than that,' I challenged.

I bit down on his throat. He would have a mark there in the morning. He knew it and pushed against my mouth, wanting more. I marked him again on the other side. He grabbed the headboard of the bed and used it for leverage, pulling himself into me at the same time he pushed. I wrapped my legs around him.

'Like this?' he gasped.

'Fuck, yes.'

I wiggled down just enough. I bit down on one of his hard, flat nipples and he gasped. My hands raked across his back. I thrust up to meet him each time. He began to lose control, a slow trembling that made him suddenly pull back and fight to regain his senses.

'Who is in charge here?' he joked, and I laughed. Then he began to laugh too, and the rhythm was broken. He rolled over on the bed and pulled me with him. Somewhere along the way his cock slipped out of me. I lay on his chest and we laughed until I was weak with the release of it.

'You really can't stand to lose control, can you?' I asked.

He slowly lifted his hands to the headboard. His fingers curled around the bottom of it.

'Show me,' he whispered.

I found the belt of my satin robe. He lay under me, placid as still water, as I tied him to the headboard. He moved his knee and I pitched forward as he chuckled. I

143

caught myself on the headboard. It made a resounding twang as it whacked against the wall.

'You are stronger than you look,' I said in amazement.

'Just didn't want you to think you had complete control,' he drawled.

'You just wait, smartass,' I taunted as I slipped down between his legs. He tensed, his whole body going rigid. Then he relaxed slowly. I sat there quietly and waited it out, knowing his curiosity would take over in due time.

And it did.

'Touch me,' he whimpered quietly.

'I didn't hear you,' I said.

'Touch me…'

'Beg me.'

He shifted on the bed and sighed. He didn't want to ask. I bent down and took him into my mouth, one long stroke that sent his hips arching up off the bed. I sucked hard all the way up the length of his shaft. He was hard as a rock, his head swollen with desire. I tasted a drop of bittersweet pre-cum as I licked the tip and moved away.

He tried to bring his hands into play, forgetting he was bound. I watched him struggle. My marks were all over his skin. He looked strong and vulnerable all at once. I watched and caressed his thighs as he slowly tested the bonds, then gave up. The look in his blue eyes was priceless. He had no choice, and the newness of that frightened him. I waited while the anticipation battled with the fear.

The anticipation won.

'Please,' he said. 'Please, please…'

'Please what?'

'Please do anything…please use me…'

Well, well. That was *much* better. My mind raced with

possibilities as I bent to his cock once again. I blew cool air over his head and made him whimper. I watched him quiver, his body reaching for me in the midnight air. My tongue traced every ridge and vein I could find. Then I delved lower and watched as his thighs began to tremble.

'More…'

I slid my teeth up his cock and he groaned loudly.

'Like that?'

'Oh, shit. Yes.'

I slid my mouth down his shaft. I worked him slowly for an eternity. His balls were heavy and tense in my hand. His thighs trembled and once he tried to pull his legs together, but I pushed them hard with my knees, keeping them open. He writhed on the bed when I slid a finger down to his ass and gently probed there.

'No,' he whimpered, but didn't pull away.

'Yes.' I pushed harder then, slipping one finger halfway inside, and he arched up. Right into my throat. I swallowed on him once and he gasped with the overload of sensation.

'I'm going to come,' he cried out desperately.

I backed off just a little, sucking him too softly to let him orgasm. He bucked up on the bed. His whole body shook with the effort of needing to come but not being allowed to do so. I suddenly sucked harder, and when he moaned I wrapped my hand around his cock and squeezed. Hard.

'Jesus Christ…*Fuck*!'

'Close your eyes.'

He did so obediently, without hesitation.

I pushed my finger deeper into his ass. I squeezed his cock harder. Then I stroked upward with both my finger and my hand, and the orgasm that hit him came so quickly

145

he had no time to prepare for it.

His voice was a deep rasp of surprise. I enveloped him with my mouth just as the first stream of semen shot from him. He bucked into me mindlessly, throwing his head back against the pillows, pulling hard on the satin bonds that held his wrists. He groaned with every pump, until he finally collapsed back onto the sheets, exhausted by the outpouring of his body.

The trembling got worse. His whole body shook as I worked my way along the length of it, finally stopping to kiss his chin and brush his hair away from his face. Wetness made a thin sheen on his temples.

'You cried?' I asked quietly.

'Yes. I think so. I don't know why.'

'You don't have to know why.'

He smiled as I slowly untied him, then kissed each red mark on each wrist. I sucked one of his fingers into my mouth and tasted it, the salt and a bit of me and a little tinge of metallic something. I took the time to explore his body, to taste the salty spot just under his collarbone, the sweet spot just inside his elbow. The strangely musky taste on his belly. He held me lightly by the hair and let me wander the roadmap of his body.

Then he pulled me up the bed and did the same to me. I lay back and reveled in the feel of his lips and tongue meandering everywhere. He tasted the most intimate places...the cleft just below the small of my back...the curve of my ankle...the little sheen of sweat under my breasts. By the time he made his way back up to my mouth, I was trembling with desire and the honesty of being discovered by someone who really knew how to explore.

'That was thorough,' I whispered shakily.

'I'm going to make love to you,' he responded. 'Then I just might fuck you.'

He lifted one of my knees, opening me just enough. He slid his cock so deeply it hurt. I knew I would be almost too sore to walk in the morning, but I didn't care. I just wanted more of him.

He moved slowly, carefully. I tried to buck up to meet him but he caught my hips and held me where I was. The impatience in me raged. I wanted more, I wanted a hard fuck, but he wouldn't let me have it. Instead he moved with an agonizing slowness that drew sensations from me I had never felt before.

'Hold still,' he said. 'Just feel. Don't have a goal. Just feel.'

'I don't know how…'

'I'll teach you.'

And teach me, he did. All I could do was feel, and that is what I did…lay under him and let him move in any way he pleased, let him find places in the depths of me that made me call his name. His hands were everywhere at once, yet calm and careful. When I thought I couldn't take anymore, he wrapped his arms around me and pulled me as close as he could. I opened my mouth against his chest and tasted the sweetness there. I breathed deeply of the scent that was uniquely him. He buried his face in my shoulder and whispered into my ear. And all the while, he never moved faster…he simply let the sensation build on its own, without the need for anything more.

But even more surprising was the feeling inside, the contentment in the midst of passion. The safety and security I felt in his strong arms. The feeling that his body above mine was the only tether I had left to the world, and that world didn't include anyone at all but the two of us.

There was no pain, no worries, no cares. There was only me and that man moving so sweetly within me.

Oh my God, I thought. *He's making love to me. This is what it's really like.*

And I began to cry softly, while he kissed each tear and never stopped moving.

It might have been a few minutes or a lifetime later, when he came inside me. The flooding warmth of his body caught fire in mine. The orgasm was the hardest one I had ever felt, but it didn't provoke me to scream out or dig my nails into his back. Instead, the sensation traveled over my whole body, replete and invigorating all at once. We stared at each other as his essence emptied out into me, filling me and spilling out onto the sheets below us. The throbbing of my body seemed to pull him inside, greedy, wanting as much of him as I could keep for myself.

After long moments he moved away, just enough to collapse beside me. He held me in his strong arms and kissed my forehead, then my face, then my lips.

'That…'

'Shh. Hush, girl.'

'But…'

'You don't have to say it. I know.'

I stopped trying to articulate things I couldn't begin to explain. I turned into him and pulled him close, my hands sliding into his hair. He rested his head on my breast and I could almost hear him counting the heartbeats as our bodies descended from the pinnacle of passion. His foot caught the back of my leg and he pulled me even closer. I smiled and kissed his forehead, running my hands through the blond strands over and over.

Some time later I awoke. It was a delightful wake-up call…his body sliding deep into mine. I reached behind

148

me and placed my hand on his hip, feeling him move slowly.

'You're awake,' he teased.

'Somewhat.'

'Get on your knees and I'll wake you up in style.'

I giggled and rolled onto my knees. I pushed back against him, my body still warm with sleep, my limbs stretching with a pleasurable ache. I felt sore in places I had forgotten could get that way. He slid deep and I almost winced.

'Hurt?'

'A little…not bad, though.'

'We need to slow down,' he sighed mockingly.

'Don't you dare think about it,' I shot back with a grin.

'As I recall,' he said with a contemplative air, 'I owe you a fuck.'

I laughed and pushed back against him. He took a handful of my hair and pulled. Gently at first, then harder as he felt me grow wet around him. He thrust in and out with shallow motions, just enough to make me want more.

'Tell me you want it,' he growled.

'I want it. Oh, I want it…'

'You want it hard? You want it all at once?'

'Yes…'

He thrust hard, almost lifting me off the bed. I cried out with the power of it.

'Show me how strong you really are,' I gasped in invitation.

He drove hard into me, and I had to brace myself against the headboard to keep from hitting it. He was harder than he had been earlier in the night. And I was tighter. He began to pump into me, with little finesse and with one goal in mind: to make us both come.

149

I reached under me and touched my clit. He moaned that it made me tighter. I reached farther and felt his cock sliding in and out of me, touched his balls as they pressed against my mound. Then I went to work on my clit again, driving myself to an orgasm that just might make him come, too.

Then he was kneeling behind me, fucking me harder.

'Are you okay?' he asked between tortured breaths.

'I'm okay. Let go of me. Let me see what you can do…'

And so he did. He fucked me as hard as he could, as hard as any man had ever fucked me, so hard that my pussy burned. He drove straight in and out, his hands on my hips holding me steady for his thrusts. He fucked me so hard I had to bite my lip to keep from screaming. It was agony and torture and *oh my God* it was good, and before I knew what was happening I was coming on his cock, coming so hard he almost had to stop moving. Nothing in the world mattered but that man fucking me until his body exploded.

He came with a shout that sounded almost painful. I felt him flood me again, and this time he didn't stop, but kept moving so that our bodies made a wet sound every time he thrust. I collapsed under him as he finally slowed and found the limits of how far his body could be pushed. One last time and he held there until he went soft and gently slipped out of me.

I lay on the bed, completely satisfied and too out of breath to speak.

He took my hand, kissed it, and placed it on his heart. I snuggled up to him as he lay down beside me. I felt safe and warm and completely enjoyed.

'We are going to pay for all this tomorrow,' he

whispered, and I smiled. He kissed my closed eyelids, one at a time. He pulled me close, his hair falling over my head as he kissed my temple. The quilt fit just right around our bodies, closing out the coldness of the early morning.

'Tell me I don't have to go home,' he whispered.

'I want you to stay.'

'I'll bring you breakfast in bed,' he offered hopefully.

'You are breakfast, dear.'

He chuckled lightly, already drifting off to sleep. His breathing became low and steady. I let my eyes drift closed and felt myself moving toward sleep. I lay cocooned in his arms, knowing it was a new beginning.

And I wondered how the hell I was going to walk in the morning.

Flying
by Paige Roberts

Flying. It's the greatest gift that I have ever received, even though it came along with this curse of living in darkness and craving the lifeblood of others. Some would say the greatest gift of my life is eternal youth, but there are times when I wonder if immortality in darkness and hunger is as much a curse as the rest. But flying. Flying is what I live for, purest joy and freedom. I can feel the soft night air caressing my naked skin and playing with my long thick hair, and I laugh aloud. I fly with my arms outstretched as if to embrace the wind. From below, I might seem a willing sacrifice on the starry altar.

But I do not fly just for the pleasure of it now. Hunger drives me. Need.

I do not want to seek another. I want only to be left alone with the soft air and the stars, but I must have the warmth of life to survive.

I fly toward the edge of the wilderness where civilization brushes against it and forest gives way to fields fenced with barbed wire, wishing for solitude, but searching for warmth, my eternal conflict of desire versus need. My eyes watch for the bright flickers of life. I see the warm red silhouette of an owl swooping on a mouse in a field, a fellow hunter seeking life in the darkness.

I need something larger. I can feed on a deer or a cow or a horse and it will keep me alive for another night. It does not truly feed the need, quench my desire, but it quiets the hunger for a time, until finer, more elusive prey can be found. The hunting ground I have chosen has little of the tastiest game, but there are none of my own kind here, whose company I abhor, and who would seek to fight me for what game there is. I prefer the peace and solitude, even if it means I must use greater cunning to find prey, and patience, so much patience.

I see a flicker of movement on the edge of the trees, a deer. I swoop down like the owl on the mouse, but I sheer off at the last moment and land in a crouch in the grass. The doe bounds away, her tiny fawn beside her. I will not take the life of the mother, and leave the babe orphaned. There is other prey. Tonight, perhaps, the finest prey, if I have calculated correctly.

I kick free of the earth and ride the soft wind once more above the trees. There. Horses. I have fed from this herd before. Horses are large enough that I can feed from one without ending its life. I prefer that whenever possible.

I land feather light on the back of one of the larger of the beasts. It's a male. I can tell by his scent. At first, he is startled and runs, but I pour my will through my hands as I ride him and he slows, and finally stands quivering, excited, frightened, but wanting what my hands promise.

'I will give you pleasure, beast. My kiss is bliss,' my hands promise.

And as his friends desert him, running for their lives from the dark predator out of the sky, I keep my promise. Warm life from his great pounding heart fills my mouth and fills the hollow place in my body. My blood, like air, is thin and cool and lifeless each night when I awaken. The beast's blood thickens me and gives me strength, solidity, warmth – life. My eyes close, and I share the bliss I feel with the beast, a gift to ease the guilt of what I must steal. I lose myself in the pleasure of feeding. It is a pale imitation of feeding on the bright life of a man, but this does no one harm. Even the beast will live, although weakened.

I hear a resonant boom and feel as if I have been struck a great blow on the side. I lie on my back on the grass, still somewhat lost in the fog of feeding and confused by what has happened. The bright warmth of some of the blood I have stolen flows out of me from a gaping hole in my side where the ribs meet softer flesh. The blood is red with warmth to my night vision, a burning dark red like the embers of a fire, molten lava oozing from inside me. I have a moment of wonder to see such an ugly wound in my body, and know that I will not die. My mind seeks to pull inside itself and seal the wound before more of the precious blood can leak away. My eyes drift closed, darkness pulling at me. So tired, must heal. I fight the pull, wondering how the wound came to be there in my flesh.

I open my eyes a slit and look up into the face of a man, young, frightened, dismayed.

'My god! You're real. You're a vampire!'

So I am. But a much damaged one. Thanks, no doubt, to the shotgun in the young man's hand. The darkness pulls again. Will he shoot me again and take my head while I sleep and try to heal? Perhaps. I could fight the healing sleep and rip his head from his shoulders instead. But, he has soft eyes, like the doe. I have seen him before, tending his horses, mending the fences, even late into the night. I watched him aid a mare in childbirth three weeks ago. His care for her was gentle, his smile bright with wonder at the new foal. I do not want his life to end. Mine? Perhaps so. Dark empty unchanging nights stretch into uncounted years behind me, and into infinity before me. If the soft-eyed man with the shotgun chooses to end it, then so be it.

I let the darkness take me and seek the inner circles of my mind where I can close the vessels to stop the loss of the precious blood. I use its life and strength to mend the damage done by fifty bits of lead. Slowly the power of the blood and my mind brings the torn flesh of my side together. I stay in the safe darkness inside my head until my skin is smooth and unmarked and my body is whole as if never damaged.

When I open my eyes, I blink in the brightness and shift from darkness to light vision. The first thing that comes into focus is a man's face, young, but careworn, crinkles around his eyes from squinting at the sun.

A campfire flickers nearby, the source of the bright light.

'You're awake! I was afraid I'd killed you,' the man says.

I shift, trying to sit up, but my hands are bound behind my back. I wiggle a bit to test my situation. My ankles are bound as well, and my ankles and wrists attached by a short length of rope. I lay still again on my side, watching my captor. He moves well, strong and sleek like the horse I tasted. He would taste far better than the horse, I have no doubt.

His eyes shift from my direct gaze and drop. 'Sorry about the ropes. But I've seen what you've done to my herd. I don't want to end up with holes in my throat and missing near half of my blood like them, or more, since I can't spare as much as a horse.'

I consider the state of my hunger. I did not lose much of the horse's blood before stopping the flow. It would not require half of the man's blood to fill me, only a pint or two. He could spare that much without harm.

I moan softly as a surge of powerful desire shakes me, just at the thought of touching this gentle man. It has been long since I tasted the mind-scrambling intensity of human blood, and even longer since I touched a man in passion, and knew I would not kill him while lost in the feeding. My sex moistens and I feel a jerk of reaction low in my belly. I want this man, so very badly. I have lived wild for so long, like an animal myself. Alone.

He comes to my side, thinking I moaned in pain. 'Are you okay?' he asks. His hand reaches out as if to touch me, but hesitates.

I moan again in anticipation, but his hand hovers over my naked skin. I can feel the warmth of it, so agonizingly close.

I can use my touch to seduce him as I did the horse, but he must touch me while I am fully conscious. I writhe a little in the bonds, allowing the flow of my thick black hair that he used to cover my breasts while I slept, to slip down, exposing my naked vulnerable body to him.

I widen my eyes, trying to look innocent and in need. I am bound. I cannot hurt you. And I desire you. Please, touch me.

'Somehow, I don't think that's a good idea,' he says drawing back.

I groan in frustration and glare at him. Damn. He is as intelligent as he is beautiful: which just makes me desire him more, if such a thing were possible.

157

He sits down in front of me, staring in wonder, immune to the fire in my eyes of anger and desire. 'A vampire! Wow. I never thought there really was such a thing. But when my horses started showing up all weak and shaky, with no mark, but two little punctures on the neck, I just had to find out for sure.'

I lick my lips, watching the way his muscles move under his skin, and deeply breathing in the scent of him. I cannot think with him so close like that. All I can do is feel. I am an aching black hole seeking to pull him in and swallow him up. I wish he would shut up and touch me.

He is still speaking to me, but I've lost track of his words. I haven't used words in years, decades perhaps. I pay little attention to the passing of time.

I try to remember words, how to speak aloud.

'Let me go,' I finally remember how to say. My voice sounds strange even to me, low and resonant and rough, like a singer after a long night.

'I can't do that, Ma'am,' the man says.

I just look at him.

He shrugs.

He fears me. Sensible, really. 'If I am not free when the sun rises, I will die,' I say softly, and again look at him with wide, innocent, and now frightened eyes.

He blinks. 'I hadn't thought that far ahead.'

'You shot me,' I point out. 'Do you want me dead?'

'No, no, I'm really sorry about that. I just couldn't see you real clear in the dark. Thought maybe it was a cougar or something after my horses. I just couldn't believe it was actually a vampire until I saw you up close.'

'You must free me, or I will die,' I say.

'And if I do cut those ropes, I'm likely to die before sunrise myself.'

158

'I will not kill you,' I say.

'I wish I could believe you,' he says.

I try to stretch a bit in my confinement and moan slightly as if in pain.

The man pulls a hunting knife from his boot and steps one leg over my body. He leans down and cuts the rope that joins my ankles and wrists.

I roll onto my back while he still stands straddling me and stretch out my full length, arching my back like a sleepy cat. My thigh brushes his leg, but his leather boots are too thick for me to affect him directly. I take a deep breath and sigh in relief at my freer movement, well aware of how that breath draws attention to my bare breasts.

The rancher swallows loudly, and I can see the hard line in his jeans. His heartbeat quickens.

'Thank you,' I say, continuing to breathe deeply. His scent is incredibly enticing.

'God, you're beautiful,' slips out of his mouth, as if he didn't mean for it to.

'Touch me,' I whisper.

'It's not...I shouldn't...'

Hunger for him pulls at me, flushing my body with trembling aching emptiness. I want him so badly, my whimper of need is real, not feigned. 'Please!' I beg.

He kneels over me and his hand reaches down toward my face. He stops a few inches away, hesitates, and starts to change his mind and draw back.

I move my head up into his palm. I kiss it and rub my cheek against it like a cat. My power flows into him through that innocent touch, and he is mine, and words are no longer necessary. Touch me. My kiss is purest pleasure. Taste me. Hold me in your arms. I know you desire me. Give in to it.

159

And he does, with an intensity that startles me. His hands are strong and sure on my body, lifting me from the ground and holding me tight against his chest as his mouth devours mine. His tongue fills my mouth, and his hand balls into a fist in the thick hair at the back of my neck.

And I begin to know what it feels like to be the prey. I moan into his mouth and melt against the strong warmth of his chest.

He hesitates, draws his face back from mine. The pupils of his eyes are dilated and dark, his mind lost in the mist of my power. He shakes his head, trying to clear it, trying with a will like iron to break free of the trap I have sprung. But his hands are still on my body, one under my shoulders, the other in my hair. I pour more power through that touch on my shoulder. I pour all the loneliness and desperate desire in my heart into his body through his fingertips. I share with him just a taste of my need, and his iron will melts away in that fire.

He groans, arches my head back by his grip in my hair, and buries his face in my throat, kissing, and licking and sucking, making me writhe in delight.

I cry out softly when I feel his teeth nip my skin, and my sex throbs with a pulse I can feel, the fresh hot blood of the horse pounding through me. I gave this man my hunger while I was bound. Now, I know how it feels to be helpless in the hands of one who wants to devour me. My body responds with a shiver of excitement, and a melting heat between my legs.

His hand slides down and finds that heat.

I whimper and shudder at the pleasure of his touch. I arch my back and lift my hips, pressing my sex against his hand, wordlessly asking for more.

His hand is strong, thick-fingered and callused. He

strokes the lips of my sex open, rough hands against tender flesh sliding in the slick hot wetness of my arousal.

Pain and pleasure mixed make me fight him, fight the ropes, fight to get closer, but it must feel like I am fighting to get away.

It excites him. His thick finger slides deep into me with little preamble, and his thumb finds the tender sensitive swollen nub and strokes it.

'Ah!' I cry out, and push my body hard onto his hand. It's not enough. More. I want far more.

His lips and tongue and teeth find their way across my collarbone and down to my breasts, and I arch my back further, whimpering and writhing and riding his hand.

'Fuck me,' I beg him. I want to feel him ride me with my hunger inside him and my wrists and ankles bound. So many times in my long lonely life I have fed on others and never known the pleasure of the prey.

He drops me to the ground, still kneeling astride me, and rips his plaid shirt off, popping buttons. The chest revealed is magnificently muscled and dusted here and there with blond to match the tousled mop on his head. His belt comes off next, and shaking hands unzip his jeans to free a long hard member swollen and thick with hot rich blood. He does not bother to remove his boots or drop his jeans any further than necessary to impale me with that swollen pole.

I can only watch panting, my arms trapped beneath me.

He grabs my thighs and shoves them open. The ropes around my ankles tighten painfully as they cross. He drives into me hard. His thickness is difficult, and he must use force to shove his staff into my resistant flesh, in spite of the abundant wetness.

Forced open, bound, and slick from my own heat, I can

161

offer no resistance.

His body bulls its way into me, forcing my tight hole to widen to accommodate it.

I whimper, nearly in tears, from the intensity of the sweet hot pleasure pain of his brutal penetration.

He ploughs into me hard and fast.

I rock my hips to match his rapid rhythm, as he drives into me to the hilt, slamming against my clitoris with each powerful thrust.

The pleasure builds rapidly in both of us toward a climax that could shatter bones.

He leans over me, his eyes frightening with my hunger and his own lust mixed. He supports his weight on one elbow, that hand caught fast in my hair and forcing me to arch back again, baring my throat and lifting my breasts high, and altering the angle of his manhood inside me until it rubs hard against my most sensitive parts with every stroke.

I can't stand it much longer. It's nearly too much.

His other hand closes on my breast in a bruising hard grip, his head dips down, and he brushes my swollen nipple with the edge of his teeth.

Too much.

Heat flows up my inner thighs like liquid iron and explodes inside me. My body spasms and bucks uncontrollably, all but throwing off my rider. I rip through the thick ropes on my wrists and ankles as if they were made of twists of paper, grab that mane of tousled blond hair, and wrap my legs around his waist, holding him tight inside me.

My fangs sink in as my body's spasms set him off. A harsh scream shouts his own pain and pleasure to the stars as he thrusts into me, even harder than before, once, twice, again, and I can feel his body jumping and spasming inside mine, and filling my sex with hot liquid life as my mouth fills with his hot blood. The taste of him is beyond glorious, and I give him my feeding ecstasy to share just as we share the soul-shaking orgasm. It is more powerful and more incredibly wonderful than anything I have ever experienced as human or vampire.

Better than flying.

When we drift back to earth. I lick the two little wounds I made, and send a bit of my healing energy into him to stop the blood flow.

I roll over onto my side, my arms cradling him gently, my legs still holding him inside me.

His mind is his own now. I no longer influence it. Tenderly, I kiss him, and he kisses me back hard. It was not just my hunger that drove him to such unbridled passion. There is a lonely need in him that nearly matches mine. When I pull back to look at him, the wonder of when he first saw me is back in his eyes.

'You could have gotten free any time,' he says softly.

'I liked being your captive,' I smile.

Shyly, he returns my smile. 'I liked it, too.'

'I told you I would not kill you.'

He chuckles. 'I guess I believe you now.'

I like his smile. It was that smile of wonder and joy of life that drew me to him. I stroke a lock of his tousled hair away from his eye.

'You sort of planned this, didn't you?' he says suddenly.

I just smile.

He chuckles again.

Reluctantly, I part from his body. Dawn is near. I must go.

I stand and he stands with me, hands reaching, both his and mine. I know I cannot stay, but I do not want this to end. Something of my sorrow must show in my face.

'Wait, take me with you, or make me like you,' he says.

'You do not wish to be like me,' I say softly, and my voice sounds lonely and raw even to me. I again brush that soft blond lock from his eye. It falls right back immediately, stubborn thing. His face is brown and his hair streaked with gold from a life in the sun. I would rather die than steal the sun from him.

'Maybe not,' he shrugs, 'But I want to be with you.'

I have already given him all the pleasures of my life. Beyond this is only loneliness and darkness. And flying. That part is good.

I smile at him and hold out my arms.

He matches my smile and moves close. I encircle him with my arms, and my dark hair enfolds him in warmth. I look into his gentle eyes, and find a peace that I have long sought and never before found. Desire and need no longer conflict within me. I can enfold him with me in my solitude, this man accustomed to the peace of the country, accustomed to the quiet company of beasts and trees.

And as I kick free of the earth to ride the soft night wind, I watch his eyes light up with wonder, and find the greatest joy of my life is even greater when shared.

Night on a Bare Mountain
by Roz MacLeod

They'd been together a couple of years, but their sex life had dwindled into routine. They'd tried sex toys, suggestions in magazines and DVDs for erotic positions, and anything short of swinging from the ceiling.

'A holiday,' Steve had said, when she had broken from him at their last attempt, 'that's what we need.'

He propped himself up on one elbow.

'My aunt owns a cottage in Dorset. The weather's still fine. Why don't I find out if she'll rent it to us for a long weekend?'

So off they went. Tess stood at the open by window of the cottage and gazed at the patchwork of fields bordered by hedges and warm stone walls. She felt very strange. Almost giddy. The white wine at lunchtime? She wasn't sure.

'Nice scenery,' she said.

Steve agreed with her.

Aunt May's stout figure blocked the doorway. 'Just come to check how you was getting on. Everything all right, me dears?'

Tess pulled herself together. 'It's great. Lovely

scenery.'

Steve pointed towards the single solitary hill dominating the surrounding fields and even the village.

'That hill looks weird. It's got trees all round it half way up and then nothing at the top.'

Aunt May moved closer to the window.

'*Bald Mount*, we call it. In olden days, the villagers used to gather up there on a midsummer night.'

'What for?' Tess asked, half suspecting she knew the answer.

'Rude goings on, so I hear. 'Tis said on that night the Lord of the Manor had his choice of fair maidens. Years ago mind you.'

Steve grinned. 'You don't say!' He rubbed his hands together. 'Seems just the spot we're looking for.'

Aunt May threw him a knowing look. 'Is that so?'

Once they were alone, Tess took off her T shirt and bra. She chose a cotton voile sleeveless shirt. It left little to the imagination and without a bra her breasts bounced like ripe melons.

While combing her hair, she glanced at Steve. He was sitting in a wicker chair, gazing out of the window.

'Penny for them,' she said, stroking his shoulders and kissing the top of his head.

Steve turned and stared at her breasts with a glint in his eyes.

'Tonight's going to be very warm.'

'Sultry,' Tess added, already guessing the drift of what he was up to, 'especially if we stay indoors.'

He leaned back, put his hand inside her shirt and pinched her nipple.

'Making love under the stars might be fun.'

He winked.

Tess felt the peculiar pricking of her flesh she'd noticed as soon as they had arrived at the cottage. And it wasn't just Steve. Every time she looked at that place, something jerked in her mind at the same time as it jerked in her pants.

They drove to a pub for dinner.

It was a spacious country inn and situated about half way between the cottage and Bald Mount. Oak beams hung across the ceiling, russet-patterned curtains matched the carpet, and the tables were laid for four. Tess poked her fork round her fish and chips, speared a chip and placed it slowly in her mouth.

'Is the food all right?'

'It's lovely. I just don't feel very hungry. It's too hot to eat.'

Steve glanced up at the whirring fan, suspended from the ceiling above their table.

'Can't you feel the breeze?'

Tess undid another button on her blouse.

A tall man was watching her from the bar. She glimpsed down at her shirt. It was practically open to the waist, her tits barely covered. She had a mad feeling she'd like to fling it off completely and throw it to the man who watched her.

'I've got such a strange sensation in my stomach,' she said.

'Do you mean excited?'

Was it excitement? 'Don't know.'

'I wonder why this pub is called *The Last Resort*?'

'How would I know? Why don't you ask one of the bar staff?'

Steve beckoned to the tall man.

The man hovered over their table. His gaze fell on

Tess's cleavage.

'It's hot,' she said by way of exclamation. The way he smiled made her clit stir under her jeans. She'd like to take those off too. Why not? It was far too hot for denims. Tough! The other customers might object. Not this man, though. Their eyes seemed to lock together.

'Everything okay for you?' he smiled warmly. His voice was like warm oil.

'Yes, thanks,' Steve said. 'We were wondering how this pub got its name?'

The man gave a wry smile. He had dark auburn hair, a healthily bronzed complexion with high cheekbones and a strong nose and chin. The badge on his white shirt read 'Alex', and underneath 'Manager'.

'There used to be a place here where villagers gathered before they went up to the hill.'

'Is it right that some pretty sexy things went on up there?' Steve was all interest.

Alex nodded. 'Right, so you've heard the story. Well not everyone was brave enough to go there, so this was their *Last Resort* for their friends and relations.'

Tess cocked her head to one side. 'Brave enough? What do you mean by that?'

'Some never came back. Some never wanted to come back.'

A sliver of ice plunged from Tess's shoulder blades and ran down her back. There was something about the way he said it and the way he looked at her that made her *feel* the intensity of his telling more keenly.

'Why?' Steve asked, sensitivity not being his forte.

'They held powerful, extreme rituals. The Mount was like a drug. People stayed. They wanted more.'

Forgetting her gaping shirt, Tess leaned forward until

her breasts spilled out of the loose cotton. She glanced down at her nipples. They were being naughty, standing out like pebbles and peeping through the opening in her shirt.

The effect was not lost on Alex. His bulging crotch thrust against his flies.

She half expected him to say something, but he didn't. Without another word, he turned his back on them and walked away.

Goose-bumps erupted all over her arms, yet the fiery stickiness in her jeans persisted. Without thinking, she raised the hem of her shirt high above her jeans and fingered the gold stud in her belly button.

'Do you still want to go there?' Steve's eyes fixed on the tantalizing strands of hair at the top of her pussy triangle, peeping over her low-slung jeans. 'By the time we get to the hill it'll be pitch black.'

Dying to set her limbs free, Tess's hands slipped to her zip as if she would tug it open to reveal her feather-like curls.

'I'll be safe enough with you,' she said, and sighed. This wasn't going to work. Their relationship was at an end and this was a last ditch attempt. Somehow she knew it was beyond redemption, and yet, she couldn't resist going up there.

The silver disk of moon and sprinkling of stars covered the hill like sequins on a velvet curtain.

'We'll walk a little way up to the first ring of trees. Even if anyone else is about, they won't see us if we bed down among the greenery.'

Steve laughed, the sound echoing round the hill.

'Shhh,' Tess warned, suddenly nervous. Silly really: the place seemed deserted and the only noise they heard was the rustle and crackle of bracken as they climbed towards the circle of oak trees.

'Here?' Steve spread the car rug on the grass.

Tess sniffed the night air. 'Can you smell that?'

Steve shrugged. 'Not really.'

'Ferns, mimosa, or is it honeysuckle? Whatever it is, it's wonderful,' she breathed.

Undoing the last button on her blouse, she kicked off her sandals and wriggled out of her jeans.

Tossing her hair, she stood naked, legs apart, her arms outstretched to the night sky, the breeze lapping her skin.

Steve made a grab at her and they collapsed to the ground together. He tried his best, but nothing much happened. She was left feeling dissatisfied, just the same as usual.

She must have fallen asleep because the next thing she felt was a fluttering movement over her left nipple. It felt quite delicious.

'Ummm,' she murmured, then jolted – a strange man knelt over her, holding a fan of leaves.

'Steve!' She looked at the sleeping figure beside her. Hadn't he heard? Steve was sound asleep.

'Tessa, don't be afraid.' The stranger held out his hand to her. 'Come with me.'

In desperation, she gave Steve a prod. 'Wake up!'

He didn't.

'Don't you want to know the secret of the mountain?'

There was something familiar about him; he was like Alex the pub manager, and yet in a way he wasn't.

The man continued, his voice deep and alluring. 'Come. I will give you exactly what you need.'

Tess hesitated. It was like being in a mist, not quite knowing where she was. She shouldn't go with the stranger and yet an inner compulsion drove her on. Was it because he'd said 'Tessa', which only her mother called her?

With one last glance at the sleeping Steve, she rose. Her body brushed against the rough weave of the man's clothing. He wore a tunic, gathered in at the waist in thick folds by a rope belt. One of her nipples caught in the threads. The man's fingers gently untangled it.

Some feeling had come with her. She began to dance, swinging her breasts at him. Oh, it was glorious to feel such freedom! Gyrating her hips, she thrust out her pelvis, kicking up her shapely legs like a can-can dancer; a mix of sweat and anticipation covering her body. There was music in her head, or was it close by?

The man held out his hand to her and she took it, noticing the sparkle of a gold ring on his right middle finger. He led her through the trees and the music grew louder – the plaintive melody of pipes, the throbbing of muted drums. Her heart beat in time to the rhythm as he brought her to the edge of the plain.

The Bald Mount was ringed with people holding aloft flaming torches. A group of naked young men and women began dancing in graceful, sensual and shadowy circles.

The men were strong and muscular, their cocks proudly thrust out, different sizes, yet all swollen and hard. 'Here,' they seemed to say, 'take mine, and mine, my one's the best.'

Girls came and slid their bodies against them.

Tess's jaw dropped. Any minute now and they would be all at it…an orgy, a real orgy of pumping, thrilling sex.

She groaned, aware of her own body responding to what was happening. Unable to stop herself, she rubbed her clit and dipped her fingers into the rich juices running

171

down between her legs.

'Come,' her companion said offering her his hand.

She needed no encouragement. She was about to fling herself into the throng of dancers when she heard a shout. The music stopped. The dancers halted. Another man stood tall against the night sky. A circlet of gold adorned his dark head. A platted chain swung round his neck and rested on his muscular chest. On his upper arm he wore a bangle coiled in the shape of a snake.

The man raised his arm. Before she knew what was happening, her companion had taken off his rope belt and bound her hands and ankles.

'What are you doing?' Her voice seemed a mile away – and small – terribly small.

Panic overwhelmed her. She struggled, but couldn't move. He picked her up and carried her to a slab of an old oak tree in the middle of the dancers. She lay prone, staring up at the night sky, her hands tied behind her like an ancient sacrifice. The music started again.

She breathed in the woody smoke of the torches.

The dancers, male and female, brushed her body with their hands as they swept by.

Some lingered, leaned over and touched her more intimately, more forcibly.

One girl fingered her clit, rubbing it in slow, delicious circles, sucking, tapping, arousing it from its long sleep.

This was not Steve. This was not a man, but still Tess cried out for more.

A handsome young man with green eyes and black hair, licked her nipples and circled his tongue round her breasts.

Another ran his penis down her stomach, playing with her labia as his handsome member lengthened against her.

She raised her knees exposing her sex and the dark

172

crack between her cheeks. If only her hands were free!

The young man sensed her desire, but did not oblige. He stood beside her, teasing her with his cock, holding it lovingly as if he longed to give it to her, she watched, open-mouthed, as he stroked his hand over his tight whorls of pubic hair.

His presence was selfish. Wrapping his hand around his penis, he pulled it faster and faster, cupped and fondled his balls, moving his fingers to squeeze the shaft so that it bulged and spurted out its abundant come in an arch over her breasts. Tess moaned. In an agony of desire, she slid off the wooden slab.

After all this, what did they mean to do with her? Fear made her kick at her ankles. To her relief, the rope slid off. Her hands still tied, heart thumping, she started to run and tripped over a tuft of grass. She tumbled and gasped, feeling a man's arms around her waist, smelling his oiled and scented skin. His fingers untied the rope at her wrists, delicately rubbing her skin to bring back the circulation.

'Tessa.'

She opened her eyes and saw his proud nose and full lips, his eyes pools of black onyx. The gold bangle in the shape of a snake rested cool against her flesh. She spread her legs around his shoulders. This might be her last day on earth, so make it a good one! 'Please,' she implored as her blood rose, her flesh quivered, and the relentless music drummed in her ears, 'please...fuck me...'

Arching his back, his hard muscles expanding, he lifted her and took her into the forest, while the noise of drums and piping faded into the distance. Quickly, he put her down, pressed her back against a tree trunk, and drove into her, deeper and deeper until she came in a rush of orgasmic frenzy.

He laid her on the grass and began sucking and licking her tender labia. She drew up her knees and took his penis in her mouth. Hungrily, she licked all round the head, tasting its salty sweetness, then ran her tongue down his shaft and sucked his heavy balls.

His hands explored her breasts, gripping her nipples, tonguing them and kneading the soft roundness of her stomach. She gasped and began to shake again, her convulsions making her thresh about in the long grass.

He raised himself, drawing his cock over her face, drops of liquid splashing onto her cheeks.

She was wanton when he turned her over, sticking out her butt, wiggling and teasing him.

She groaned as he pushed apart her plump cheeks and cried out with pleasure as he massaged her anus with sweet-smelling oil and thrust in hard.

Still inside her ass-hole, he nuzzled her neck, her ear lobes, running his fingers down her backbone, underneath and to the sticky hole of her vagina. He moaned as he jerked off and she screamed, her orgasm matching his in rhythmic intensity, her ass pumping like an automatic drill.

Eventually, satiated at last after so many months of disappointment, she collapsed onto the bed of leaves.

If she thought he was finished, she was wrong. Grabbing her hair, he pulled her round and kissed her mouth, his tongue moving like a snake inside her.

She sat astride his knees, her legs parted, full of his cock, soaked in sweat and a feeling that she could go on forever. One more climax, one more shudder of ecstasy, and suddenly everything changed.

He pulled her over him and they were rolling together, down the hill, over and over...

Was that her who screamed?

'All right?' Steve leaned over her.

Tess blinked. 'I was dreaming.' Her breasts rose and fell with breathlessness.

'Of me?'

She didn't answer and could see he didn't like it.

The moon had disappeared. She brushed the grass from her breasts and peeled off the leaves which had stuck to the inside of her legs. Unable to find her blouse, she fumbled at the zip of her jeans. Her body ached. Satisfied, yes, yet she wanted more. If only she could stay here, lie on the warm grass and watch the sun rising over the horizon – for ever. With them. With him. With whoever they were.

'Come on,' Steve said.

Suddenly she wanted to tell him, how it had been. 'I had an extraordinary dream. Did you see or hear anything or anyone else?'

'Nope. Only us.' He frowned. He liked to share things. He didn't like this.

They picked their way carefully down to the car.

Tess cupped her soft breasts to stop them swinging. The cool, fresh air invaded her senses. They'd had sex. That much was obvious. But there were two scenarios, the usual reality of tired familiarity with Steve. And the other one.

'How was it for you?' she asked.

'Much as usual,' Steve answered. 'Made a change, being in the open, though.'

Tess climbed into the passenger seat and they drove to the cottage in silence. Later they talked about their relationship. Steve opted to go back to town. She opted to say.

That night she returned to the pub.

Alex saw her. He didn't look for Steve. It was as though he already knew. He smiled.

'I knew you'd come back. That is, I hoped you would.'

She didn't know quite how it happened. Later she wondered at how fast things moved.

Once the pub was closed, he took her to his bed. Tess relaxed into the soft down of the mattress.

'What's happened?' she asked.

'We did. When you swung your beautiful boobs at me – well, that was it. Despite your boyfriend, despite the customers sitting at the bar and eating their cod and chips, I nearly wrenched off your jeans and fucked you like there's no tomorrow.'

Tess laughed. 'In front of all those people in the dining room?'

Alex entwined his legs with hers, but she caught his right hand with the band of gold around his middle finger.

She told him what had happened and about her dream.

'And definitely it wasn't you?' she said, 'the man who led me to the dancing?'

'Sadly, no.'

'Where did you get your ring?'

'It was my father's. And his father before him. Passed down in the family.'

Tess sat up. 'So now I'm a time traveler.'

Alex kissed her cunt. 'Does it matter?'

She pressed his head against her mound. 'No. It doesn't. Can I ask you something?'

'Whatever.'

'What happened after the Lord of the Manor had had his wicked way with the chosen maiden?'

'She was free to choose to have sex with a villager of

176

her choice. Anyone, everyone, as long as she liked, and no one could deny her command.'

'Is that so.' Tess smiled. 'Fuck me,' she said. 'Fuck me now.'

Mermaid by Moonlight
by Alex de Kok

It was the summer before my final year at college, and I'd
come home for the summer. Dad was working, Mom was
at home and my sister Kelly was in Europe with her
friends, a holiday before they started college in the fall.
Two years away at college had changed me a little, and I
felt restless. I felt guilty, too, as the friends I'd left behind
seemed to live in a different world to me, so I'd brought
my paints and come up to our family cottage at the lake to
do some landscapes. I'd been here for a week, and had
driven around to the mart at the main landing to stock up
on some things. By the time I got back it was just about
dark. I'd left it late in the day, else I would have used our
sailboat, as the journey by water is a lot less than the long
way round by road, although a lot slower. I stripped off
my clothes, took a quick shower, and decided to have an
early night, but it was summer, it was hot and, even tired
after the drive back, I couldn't settle in the heat. It was full
dark by now and I wandered out onto the dock, naked.
There's only our cottage in the bay and access is either by
boat or by a private back road, so I didn't fear being seen.
Anyway, what if I was? What's a naked man or two, these

days?

The moon was near full and on impulse I stepped down into the boat, hoisted the sails and cast off. It was a little cooler out on the water, but not much. The breeze was light, warm, and the boat ghosted along at a couple of knots. I knew where the hazards were and I didn't anticipate any problems. Along the bay I could see the dying glow of a campfire on one of the beaches. I could see figures moving and I watched until they were out of sight. Near the main holiday cabin area I went about. I'd sailed down on a reach and I knew I was going to have to tack back.

I was startled suddenly by a soft hail. 'Hey, Charlie!' I looked around, wondering where the call came from because sound can carry a long way over water, when I heard a gentle splashing. I peered into the darkness and could just make out a figure swimming strongly towards me. I turned the boat into the wind and the way fell off. A few strokes brought the figure to the side and a familiar face grinned at me over her hands grasping the side of the boat.

'Hi, Charlie, surprise!'

'Sally! What are you…I mean…'

'What am I doing here? Waiting for you.'

'Me? Why?'

'I recognized the boat before and guessed it was probably you. I figured you'd be coming back, so I waited, then swam out. Can I come aboard?'

'Hell, yes.' I reached out a hand to help her over the side and just about the time I remembered I was naked, saw that she was, too. The night hid my flush and I busied myself in dropping the sails. The breeze was gentle and I knew we would only drift slowly. Sally Jansen settled herself and grinned at me, comfortable in her nudity. A year younger than me, we'd known each other for ever. She'd dogged my footsteps for years, a skinny tomboy. But as we moved towards late teens and I started dating, she'd drifted out of my life.

She cleared her throat. 'Charlie, can I ask a favour?'

'Sure.'

'Are you staying at your cottage?'

'Yeah. For a week or two. Until I get fed up, I suppose.'

'Alone?'

I nodded. 'Yeah. Just me.'

'Can I stay with you until next weekend? I'll help with food costs.'

'Can I ask why?'

'Nine of us came up for the week, but the others have all paired off. I don't want to go home yet, but I feel like a spare part.' She made a face. 'All I hear is the sounds of fucking.'

I laughed, jealous suddenly. 'Yeah, you can stay. Have you got a sleeping bag?'

'Yep.'

'How about I pick you up at the main dock in the morning?'

'Great. About ten?'

'Okay. Winds permitting.'

She smiled, happy, leaning back and I took a moment just to look at her. It almost surprised me when she spoke. 'Doing anything special up here, Charlie?'

I shrugged. 'Some painting.' I let myself look at her again, silvered by the moonlight. Slim, athletic, beautiful. Emboldened by the dark I said, 'I'd like to paint you, just like that.'

Time stopped, and I held my breath, while she just looked at me for a long moment. 'Nude?'

I took a deep breath, and a chance. I nodded. 'Yes.'

Another pause, and when she spoke her voice was soft. 'Can you paint me so that no-one will recognize me?'

'Easily.'

'Okay, then.' She grinned, then sobered. 'How's Nancy?'

'It's over. She's gone off to the West coast to try to make it as an actress.' My ex. I missed her glorious body, her zest for fucking. I'd realized I wouldn't miss her pea-sized brain.

'I'm glad,' Sally said quietly.

My heart leaped and life began to look good again. Sally stood, glorious in the moonlight.

'What else are you doing besides painting?'

I shrugged.

Sally grinned. 'I'm sure we can think of something,' she said and dived neatly over the side. I stared after her until she disappeared in the dark, then laughed, hoisting the sails, beating back to the cottage.

I was early next morning, not long after nine-thirty, but she was there on the dock waiting for me, rucksack and bedroll beside her, slim and attractive in tank-top and shorts, battered sneakers, bare legs. Long, bare, legs. She waved when she saw the boat and I could see her smile from a hundred yards away. She grabbed the prow as I closed the jetty, but I wasn't worried about another ding on our battered old boat. Dad and I made sure she was watertight, and that the rigging was sound. Apart from that, the boat was a tool. A fun tool, to be sure, but a tool.

'Morning, Charlie. You're early.'

'So are you.'

182

Sally made a face. 'Caroline and Blake were half-way down each other's throat. I thought I'd get away early.' She laughed. 'I'll bet they were fucking before I reached the dock.'

'Blake Thurman?' Sally nodded. I frowned. 'Caroline?'

'Oh, right, I forgot you'd been away. Caroline Hendrix. She and her folks moved into the old Foulkes house, about six months ago.'

'Right. I see. I thought I didn't know any Carolines. You ready?'

'Am I ever. Take me away from this place!'

A couple of minutes later, her bag and bedroll safely aboard, we pushed away from the jetty and I hoisted the jib, letting it pull us away from the other boats before I hoisted the main. The wind had shifted a little and was on the beam. We made good time, so, an hour after I picked her up, Sally stepped onto our dock, looking around curiously as she'd never been before. I'd brought Nancy up a couple of times but she had no interest in the place and we'd spent most of the time in bed. Not that I was complaining, as Nancy was a Grade-A fuck, but I was pleased she'd tired of me before I tired of her. That way, we parted friends. Nancy tended to nurse grievances. Whatever, I wished her well.

'Where am I sleeping, Charlie? I'll park my bag, if that's okay? Then, maybe a swim?'

'Sounds good. Inside, second door on the left. Want a coffee before you swim?'

'After would be better.'

'Okay, I'll wait out here, get some air.' I strolled back out onto the dock, just enjoying the day. I wasn't sure what Sally had meant when she said, 'we can think of something,' but I was hoping she meant something intimate. Whatever, she was pleasant to look at, and good company, I remembered, so I was pleased to have her with me, even if it was platonic.

'Charlie?' she called from the cottage.

'Yeah?'

'Can anyone see us here?'

'Not unless they have a key for the gate. It's a private road. The only other access is by boat, and there are none even in sight. Why do you ask?'

'Because I'm naked,' she said, stepping out onto the dock. I stared, I couldn't help it, and Sally flushed, but she didn't turn away or try to hide herself. 'You said you wanted to paint me nude, Charlie. Remember?'

'I remember,' I said. 'Sally, you were beautiful in the moonlight last night, but here, now, in daylight, I think you're the loveliest sight I've ever seen.'

She grinned, the flush fading. 'What, including Nancy?'

I nodded. 'Including Nancy.' Sally was stunning, no two ways about it. She's tall, and slender. Slim waist, slim hips, but unmistakably female in the shape of her ass. Her tits aren't particularly big, but they're beautifully shaped, riding high on her chest, two lovely handfuls. Her nipples were erect, I noticed. She'd loosened her habitual ponytail and her hair curled loosely about her shoulders, the dark red matched by the curly tangle between her legs, trimmed to her bikini line.

'Charlie, you're staring. Stop it.'

'Sorry, Sally, but you're too lovely to ignore.'

She grinned, a quick flash that lit her face. 'I don't want you to ignore me, I want you to paint me. You sowed the seed in the boat last night. I want to see what I look like in your painting. I know you can paint, I've seen your work,

184

remember?'

'Yes, I remember.'

'Well, then?'

'I thought you wanted a swim?'

'I do. I thought you wanted to paint me nude?'

I laughed. 'I do, but I'm not even sure yet just how I want to pose you. Sally, you're here for almost a week, longer if you want. Let me think about it. But for now, swim?'

Sally nodded. 'Swim.' She grinned again, playful. 'You get naked, too, and I'll stay naked.'

It was my turn to flush, because my body was reacting to her unclad beauty, and my erection was growing. 'You sure you want to see my unlovely carcass?'

She nodded. 'You've seen me, it's only fair that I get to see you, too.'

'You saw me last night.'

'Not properly, it was too dark. *You* could see *me*, because I was in the moonlight, but *I* couldn't see *you*, because you had your back to the light. Come on, Charlie, get 'em off!'

It's not as if I was wearing much, because I wasn't. Shorts and a t-shirt. I'd left my boxers off because of the heat, so undressing took me about three seconds. My prick was half-hard, and Sally's eyes fixed on it as my shorts fell around my ankles. I looked at her, and her eyes came to mine, a spot of colour in her cheeks. She smiled, her eyes warm.

'Nice, Charlie.'

I managed to swallow past the huge lump in my throat, and held my hand out. 'Swim?'

She nodded. 'Swim.' She paused. 'Charlie,' she said softly, 'if it helps, you might like to know that I'm

185

soaking.' She turned, ran lightly along the dock and dived into the lake. I stared after her, then grinned to myself. The week was looking good. I ran, and followed her into the water.

We swam for a while, just enjoying the cool water, and each other's company, too. At least I was enjoying having her there, and she seemed pleased to be with me. We'd probably been in the water about a half-hour before we hauled ourselves up onto the dock and sat side by side with our toes in the water.

'Best not sit here too long,' I said. 'Sun's hot, and I don't want you burned.'

'Charlie,' she said. 'As there are just the two of us here, do you mind if I sunbathe naked? I'd like to get an all-over tan, if I can.'

'One of the loveliest girls I know asks if she can be naked around me, and I'm supposed to object? Get real, Sally. Of course you can. I like to be naked myself, especially in this heat, so if you don't mind?'

'Not me. We'll have our own little nudist club. Exclusive membership. Just us.'

'Sounds good to me. I promised you coffee. Want some? Or a cold drink? There's sodas and beer in the fridge.'

'Too early for beer, too hot for coffee. A soda sounds good.'

'Help yourself.'

She laughed. 'Hey, I just got here, remember? I don't even know where your fridge is!'

'Oops. Come on, I'll show you.' The cabin wasn't huge. A big living-room that covered most of the front, south-facing for the sun, a porch and deck shading the windows. Kitchen at one end, with a dining annex.

Propane stove and refrigerator. Two bedrooms. A double that I was using, as I liked the room, and a smaller room with twin bunk beds to which I'd directed Sally, with a bathroom between the bedrooms. Simple, but comfortable.

I took a couple of sodas from the fridge and turned to Sally. She'd come closer than I realized, silent on bare feet and as I turned, we collided. She grabbed my arm to stop herself falling, recoiled, and was suddenly leaning against me, breasts against my arm, her face bare inches away, staring into my eyes. I paused a moment, then bent towards her, slowly, giving her time to turn away. I saw a smile come into her eyes and as I bent, she lifted her lips to mine.

The kiss was gentle at first, as we learned each other's taste, until Sally broke it. A protest died unspoken as she took the sodas from me and put them on the bench, hung her arms around my neck and moved back into the kiss. It was hotter this time, lips parted, breathing each other's air, tasting each other's mouth, a heat building in us to match that growing in my groin, my erection thickening as the naked girl in my arms pressed against me. I moved awkwardly, but she pushed hard against me for a moment and then broke the kiss, a soft smile on her face as she gazed at me.

She nodded. 'Yes, Charlie. Before you ask, the answer is yes.'

'You're sure?'

'Certain. I was last night, as soon as you told me about Nancy. God, I was so jealous of her!'

'Jealous? Whatever for?'

Sally fixed me with a look. 'Because she was in your bed and I wasn't.'

'Not any more,' I said, a jolt of pure pleasure running

187

through me.

'You mean, she isn't, or I am?'

'You are, if you want to be.'

Sally smiled. 'I do. Now?'

I bent and scooped her up, her startled squeak in my ears as I turned towards the bedroom. I kissed her. 'Now is good. In fact, now is excellent.'

In the bedroom, I laid her on the bed and stretched out beside her, propped on my elbow. I rested my hand on her belly for a moment and she smiled, reaching for it, moving it up. Her breast was soft, but firm, yielding, but pushing against my hand, the nipple a hard thrust against my palm. I stroked her, delighting in the smooth softness of her skin, bending across to lick and kiss her nipple. She shuddered when I took her nub between my teeth, her hands in my hair, dragging my head up so that we could kiss again. Without breaking the kiss she lifted my hand from her breast and pushed it down, and I let it move down across her belly and into the tangle at her fork.

I could feel her heat and, now, I could smell her excitement. I let my fingers slip down, into the heat and wet between her legs. Almost unconsciously, I think, she moved her legs apart, breaking the kiss, staring wide-eyed at me as I brought my fingers to my nose to smell her readiness, and then to my lips to taste the salty-sweetness of her.

'I told you I was soaking,' she whispered. 'Now, Charlie, please? Now?'

I moved to kneel between her legs, my erection hot and hard before me. There was only welcome in her eyes as I moved to enter her, and a soft gasp as she felt me push into her. I moved in only a little, and then pulled back to spread her juices, pushing back again, further this time,

188

wondering, but there was no obstruction, no resistance, and I felt a brief pang of jealousy at whoever had come before me.

It was almost as if she had read my mind, because she shook her head, her smile soft and warm. 'My dildo, Charlie. I popped my own cherry, with my dildo,' she whispered, holding my eyes with hers. 'I pretended it was you, and I wanted to be ready for when you were free to love me.' She stretched up to kiss me. 'You're my first, Charlie. I waited for you, because I knew one day you'd see me as a woman.'

'I don't know what to say.'

She smiled, shaking her head. 'No words needed, Charlie. Just fuck me, love me, fill me.' I think she read my mind again. 'Fill me, Charlie, I'm safe.'

I was deep in her now and I began to move, pulling back until I almost left her, then pressing back into her, feeling her tight around me, and as I moved her juices spread and I moved more easily, relishing the slick, hot tightness of her, enjoying the slither of my prick in her, smelling her, that rich aroma of superheated woman ready for her lover, a film of sweat building between us at our join in the summer heat, the sound of our joining audible in the quiet of the bedroom.

Sally was breathing quickly, almost a pant, and as I thrust into her, withdrew, thrust again, her breathing modulated until it was in time with my thrusts. There was sound in her breathing, and I realized she was saying, 'yes, yes, yes,' as I thrust into her, almost inaudible. Her eyes were closed, her hands on my shoulders, and I changed the angle of my penetration slightly, increasing the friction, my thrusts even more audible now, the sweat beading both of our brows.

It couldn't last. It didn't. Sally's breathing was a gasp now on each stroke, the almost inaudible 'yes' clear now, a cry in my ears as I felt that bone-deep, soul-deep, almost-ache that goes before climax building in me, but before I could warn Sally I felt her pussy clamp down on my prick, she gave a tight scream, and then she was shaking in the turmoil of her climax, the clutching contractions of her bringing me over the brink to feel my hips jerk in reflex, in that miniature death that is orgasm, my climax shaking me, my prick driving into Sally in mindless response to the milking clutch of her.

Gradually, slowly, we stilled, sweat wet between us at our join, two sets of lungs straining to extract oxygen from the air. Sally opened her eyes and stared up at me, a smile in her eyes spreading to her whole face. She stretched up and gave me a quick kiss.

'Wow,' she said.

I laughed, and nodded. 'Wow is good. I can go with wow.'

'Worth waiting for, Charlie, but I'm spoiled now. I didn't know what I was missing, but now I do and I want it again.'

I kissed her. 'That makes two of us, sweetheart.' I eased my position slightly, but I knew I couldn't stay with her much longer. 'Better ease out before I fall out.'

Sally pouted. 'Come back soon, then.'

'I will.' I eased back and flopped to my back beside her. We sprawled together, relaxed in the afterglow of good sex. I'd thought Nancy was good, and she was, but I was realising that sex with Nancy had been for Nancy first, me second, where, even after only one experience, I knew Sally wanted it good for both of us. I glanced across at her and she smiled and blew me a kiss.

190

'I could just drop off to sleep,' she murmured.

'Why not?'

She smiled. 'Any thoughts on the painting?'

'Yeah, I have. You want me to paint you so you can't be recognized, right?'

She grimaced. 'I guess. Not so much for me. I've seen your work, and I think you'll make me look good enough I'd be proud to be recognized. It's my Dad. He'd flip. I think Mom would be okay, but not Dad.'

'Okay. Not a problem. I've always thought that the curve through the waist into the hip of a reclining nude, either from in front or from behind, is one of nature's loveliest curves, so do you want me to paint you from behind, or from the front?'

She laughed. 'Both! From the front, for you. From behind, for your portfolio. Okay?'

'Very okay. Turn over, get comfortable. Fall asleep if you want. I'll take a couple of photos with my digital camera, and I'll get my sketch pad.'

'And when you want a break? What then?'

I knew the answer she wanted. 'We make love again.'

Sally smiled; warm, loving. 'Good,' she said.

Starring Tonight
by Kitti Bernetti

Funny how sometimes your fantasies catch up with you.

With me it's always been fancying the unattainable. When I was a boy in school, eleven years old with trousers that looked as if they'd had a row with my ankles and a blazer that was tailor made for King Kong, I fancied Casey Blackwell. I didn't just fancy her, I obsessed about her twenty-four hours a day. It wasn't because of her fully formed breasts and those come-and-get-it eyes although they helped some. It was because she was sixteen and I was about as likely to get off with her as I was to become President of the United States. Hah, and they say women are fickle.

Now I'm older, six foot four and not a pimple in sight. If I looked up Casey she'd probably fall at my feet with a bad dose of younger man syndrome. Except if she did that, I wouldn't want her. How things change. Except I don't. I still fancy women who I'm about as likely to sleep with as the world is to stop turning. Take the lady lawyer who handled my divorce. Those brains sure came gift wrapped. Eyes as blue as the flash on a jay's wing but a look as cold as marble even in the middle of a heat wave. I know it's not really done to lust after your divorce lawyer when you're meant to be all cut up about the end of a beautiful marriage. But getting out of my marriage was a relief for both of us. Married too young, we'd given it ten years before we finally bought ourselves a one-way ticket out.

I suppose that's one of the reasons I'm now sitting in this hotel room on the outskirts of a city I can barely pronounce. I've done a good day's business, sealed some deals and the adrenaline's pumping but I've got nowhere to take it. I'm lying back on a green coverlet that's seen enough strangers to fill the Yankee stadium, with a calling card in my hand that I've been nursing for the past two hours, wondering if I dare pick up the phone. You gotta understand me. I have never done anything like this in my life. I was always faithful to my wife. I don't believe in betrayal, I could have coped with telling her had I been going out with another gal but I never did, not once. But now I'm free and I'm in a place that's making me feel as horny as a sailor in port with a one night pass.

Do you believe in coincidences? I didn't until five minutes ago but I do now. You see, for me the ultimate turn-on would be a night with a film star. Not like they make them today, all emaciated and doe-eyed, like greyhounds on speed. I like my film stars fifties-shaped with curves you could send a roller coaster down and hair so blonde there'd be no way those curls came from anywhere other than out of a bottle.

Marilyn, she is my ultimate. Marilyn Monroe; just saying that name, rolling it around on my tongue makes me a little hard. She surely is not just the most beautiful, sexy thing on two legs, she's a legend, and when it comes to the unattainable that's a real turn on for me.

Which just about explains why, for the first time in my

life I'm thinking of paying for my kicks: You see the service on offer on this little card I'm twirling between my forefinger and my thumb is something way out of the ordinary. I've never paid before, never needed to. I'm not given to brag, but I'm not a bad-looking guy. I work out each day no matter which hotel room I'm in and I eat good food. Being on the road means it's easy to eat trash but I don't. I'm a lean steak and salad guy, a water ice and fruit guy. I guess it shows in a clear skin that tans easy thanks to my Sicilian ancestors.

Why am I stalling? I guess it's because calling up a girl for sex and paying her is just way out of my rule book. 'Specially if she looks as much like Marilyn as the girl on this card looks. 'Starring Tonight', that's the name of the escort agency. 'Hollywood look-alikes' says the blurb. More like starlets who haven't made it but have to do something to earn a crust. Marilyn's on the front, but there on the back are Vivien Leigh, Marlene Dietrich, Mae West. All fine, fine-looking women and so like the real thing. But my fantasy come true is Marilyn. If she isn't available I'll go for a run, take a cold shower and if that doesn't drive my animal urges away, I'll go in for a little solitary arm wrestling. Only the best, the most unattainable will do for me.

I pick up the phone and dial.

'Hello, can I help you?'

I hesitate and shake my head in disbelief. That voice, small, breathy like a child's but not like a child's at all. They've certainly done a fantastic job of making her sound like Marilyn. That girl must've worked with a voice coach until her larynx could do press-ups.

'Is that Marilyn?' I ask.

'Sure,' she says with a little giggle, 'who else would it

195

be? It was me you wanted wasn't it?'

'Why yes, as a matter of fact it was. Are you…are you free tonight?'

'Of course. Just give me your address and I'll be right over.'

It's as easy as that. Suddenly I'm all fingers and thumbs puffing up cushions on the couch I haven't even sat on and straightening the bedspread. I know in my heart of hearts she won't really look like Marilyn, that I'll have to keep the lights down low and play games in my head to conjure up the real thing. I don't like to close my eyes when I'm making love but if I just listen to that voice my imagination will fill in where her make-up hasn't quite done the trick. There's a knock on the door. I walk over, putting on my tie and wondering whether to humour the girl on the other side of the door in her act. Maybe it turns her on too to pretend to be someone else. Don't be stupid, I chastise myself. This is a working girl, they don't get turned on. Their job is to make sure you're in that state. She wouldn't have to work that hard. I was already three-fifths gone just thinking about her.

I open the door. There in the half light of the dim passageway is the most superb vision of ripe womanhood I have ever had the pleasure to drink in. She is wearing an off the shoulder white dress which is either staying up by pure magic or maybe it's that magnificent shelf of breasts which is helping it defy gravity. The fabric, sheer and ruched is not so much see-through as designed to magnify the female form. It clings lovingly to every contour like shrink wrap over a packet of pears. Underneath it I can make out perfect girl-curves. Round, upright, pert. She has that turn-on combination of luxurious and tarty at the same time.

I have to tear my eyes away from her body to look up at her face. This is unbelievable. I gasp and my hand drops from the handle of the door – I no longer have the power to hold on. She is the spitting image of Marilyn. The word 'doppelganger' comes to mind. I once had a friend who swears to this day that he saw a girl standing on a station platform across the tracks from him who worked in the same office. He waved and called out her name but she didn't bat an eyelid, instead stepping onto the train and disappearing. When he got to work he phoned her to find out why she snubbed him only to discover she was on holiday in a different continent. He can still hardly believe her but he does believe now that everyone has a double. And looking at this girl, so do I. Her mouth quivers in a perfect 'O', glistening with come-hither red lipstick. The eyes are heavy-lidded and half shut and painted with black eye-liner. Brows plucked into a bowed curve give her a wide-awake beckoning look which she turns on me like car headlights blinding an alley cat.

'Aren't you going to invite me in?'

There's that voice again: that unusual careful enunciation of every word that comes from shaping her lips in that studied oh-so-Marilyn way. My knees threaten to give way as I move aside and watch in sheer admiration as she sashays across the room. Her rump reminds me of a prize racing horse I once saw at a meet. Proud and upright, the cheeks encased in the clingy white material bob up and down as if they are on a choppy sea. Mesmerized I watch her turn and sit on the bed. I thought I was smitten until I saw her wink at me. Now I'm devastated. A slow lazy all-knowing wink, those extra long lashes brush against the silken skin of her face. Mesmerized, I wonder if maybe she's had plastic surgery to work this miracle-double thing. Then I think what the hell, stop looking for the joins and just enjoy yourself.

'Sit down big boy.' She says pouting.

I forgive her the cliché, I would forgive her anything.

'You're gorgeous,' I know it's a ridiculous thing to say but it slips out, it has to be said. It is sooooo true. I sit on the spot where she's patted the bed and watch her cross those lightly tanned legs giving me a glimpse of thigh where the white skirt splits. I once saw a film where Cyd Charisse danced with Gene Kelly. Every time he swirled her round you caught a sight of pure, figure-hugging simple white knickers encasing a bottom as round as a ripe apricot. It was coy, it was calculated. I thought it was one of the sexiest things I'd ever seen until I sat next to this girl uncrossing and crossing her legs. I just know she has the same sort of knickers on as I catch the tiniest glimpse. I swear I've died and gone to heaven.

Marilyn reaches out, picks up my hand and places it on her thigh. 'You look so much like,' I began, 'like Marilyn. How come you aren't in the movies or something –?' I'm blurting. She takes one crimson painted finger and places it on my lips. Then she leans over, thrusting her breasts against me and whispering in my ear.

'Sometimes it's better just to lie back and accept rather than to question. I'm having a good time. I hope you're having a good time. Isn't that enough?'

As I run my hand up her thigh, displacing the material of her skirt I nod, struck dumb. It sure is. As I feel her hand cup the back of my head and draw me to her I close my lips around hers and feel her mould to my mouth. As I breathe in I smell the unmistakable Chanel No5 scent filling my nostrils. As if I'm falling into a chasm I feel myself collapse onto the bed as she pulls me downwards.

We kiss and she allows me to slowly push the dress further down her shoulders. 'I want to see you,' I say. 'Stand up. Please.'

She smiles, is it because of the politeness I cannot help using in front of this goddess? Whatever it is, it does the trick. Obligingly she stands up in front of me while I lounge on the bed, staring at the superb vision before me as she pushes the dress with a little wiggle of her ample hips, down over her waist, dropping it to her ankles. She is wearing white peep-toe court shoes with high heels and nails painted so they sparkle in the half-light. She steps neatly away from the lifeless dress. Without her it is like the shapeless husk of a caterpillar once the butterfly has escaped. I was right. She stands in trim, waist high knickers which cover a girlishly flat stomach, the perfect foil to the plumpness of her rear. I raise my eyes and see that she was bra-less under the dress. Her creamy white gloriously ample breasts seem to glow. She bows her head forward, letting the blonde cloud of curls dip over her eyes then, raising her arms, she puts her hands behind her head collecting her hair. She lifts her face and pouts. I swear she's enjoying every minute as she strikes the perfect model fifties pose, with one foot on tiptoe in front of the other and a smile that says come and get it.

Unable to wait any longer, I find my feet, stand up, put one hand underneath her and lift her laughing onto the bed. One minute I am over her, covering her in hungry kisses. The next she sits over me, her blonde hair tickling my chest, those lidded eyes locked into mine. I push her gently down, hook my finger over the tight white knickers and ease them down over her hips, smiling as I notice she is definitely a natural blonde. Hard and eager I cannot wait any longer but ease myself into her, feeling her enfolding her arms around me. I feel a build up in my aching crotch like I have never experienced with any other woman. My heart is pounding as I feel the blood surge through me. Suddenly I am Superman and Action Man. I am Julius Caesar and the whole damn Holy Roman Empire marching to victory I feel so sexually potent in her grasp. My muscles tense like I am lifting the weight of twenty men. I look into those liquid eyes as they appraise me and blink slowly like a cat's. In a burst of fulfilment I explode, causing her to shudder and sigh with a sound which tells me that she knows the power she has over me and enjoys it.

Leaving me on the bed, collapsed like a soldier after battle, she gets up and puts first her dress then her shoes back on.

'You're not going are you?' I sit up, desperate to keep her for as long as possible. 'Stay, please stay and talk to me, I want to know more about you. I'll pay whatever it costs.'

I watch her walk towards the mirror as she straightens her hair and I jump up, clutching the still warm sheet around me.

'You're sweet. I can't stay,' she says, the pink lips even more beautiful for being devoid of lipstick, the bouffant hair even more lovely now it is flatter. She is standing with her back to me. I stand up wanting to look at her face in the mirror, when my jaw drops.

The only reflection I see is my own. I'm standing in an empty room. She turns around to look at me, blows me a kiss and says, 'I'm really sorry I can't stay.'

Dumbstruck, I watch her step through the solid wall as if it were nothing more than a beaded curtain and I am left alone.

Brushing Flesh
by J. Carron

The Detective Chief Inspector's in a foul mood when they enter his office. He draws heavily on a cigarette, even although prominent signs on the door indicate it's a no-smoking office. The grey pall fills the tiny airless room. DI Claire Reid tries hard to conceal her disapproval. But the boss notices the lines of displeasure etched across her face.

'It's one of the few vices I've got left, okay?' he snorts harshly. 'Now take a seat.'

There's only one free chair and her sidekick Danny knows better than to make a move for it. She doesn't sit comfortably, knowing nothing good ever comes of an early morning invitation to the DCI's office.

'Bloody Eastern Division,' the boss mutters. 'They've landed a right one on my desk. They want two of my officers to go undercover on their patch. Obviously they think we've nothing better to do down here than help them out.'

'You want us to do it?' she guesses.

'No I don't, but I don't have any choice,' the DCI barks.

He tosses a brown envelope across the desk.

'Art theft,' he explains.

Claire opens the envelope and slips a sheaf of glossy photographs out. She raises her eyebrows as she examines the first picture.

'That was my first reaction,' the DCI mumbles.

Danny cranes his neck to get a look.

'Dirty pics,' he chuckles enthusiastically.

The photo shows a painting of a naked woman reclining, plump legs spread, arms behind her head. Claire notices how exaggerated her features are, large and voluptuous breasts, a bold red vagina, the swelling labia pink and protruding, framed by a mesh of wiry pubic hair.

She feels her face redden.

'Not what I'd choose to hang over the fireplace,' the DCI continues, 'but apparently they're worth thousands and they've been stolen.'

'So what do you want us to do?' Claire asks.

'Eastern Division have had no luck so far. I want you pair to pose as collectors of erotic art. Your first stop will be the artist's studio.'

'I didn't think we'd have to pose as a married couple,' Danny huffs as they motor through glorious open countryside. He works his way through the photographs, examining each one in detail and making lurid comments as Claire drives.

'The feeling's mutual,' she mutters.

She isn't sure if she'll be able to carry the pretence off. Danny's amiable enough but he's not her idea of perfect husband material. He carries too much weight and has too many irritating little habits. That said, she hasn't yet found a man who is.

At least he isn't clad in polyester today. He's swapped his usual ill-fitting suit and garish tie for something rather more casual and she's done likewise. Eastern Division loaned them a shiny new Mercedes convertible to help carry off their cover story. She's beginning to enjoy the job.

Claire spots the entrance to the studio and hauls the car off the main road into a gravel courtyard at the heart of a tasteful barn conversion. The wheels crunch to a halt next to a Range Rover.

'He's obviously making money at it,' Claire observes.

Danny smiles broadly. 'I hope he's got a model or two in the studio today.'

Claire knows it's only a matter of time before he starts dribbling.

To her partner's obvious delight there is indeed a model in the studio. Claire notices his wide eyes alight on the gorgeous brunette as Marcus McIntyre ushers them into his chaotic workspace.

The girl is standing stark naked on a platform in the centre of the room, her pose provocative. She isn't a perfect ten but looks comfortable and confident with her fuller figure. She is a delectable creature, with a super sexy body and curves in all the right places.

McIntyre, on the other hand, is decidedly less easy on the eye. He's overweight and oily, a bit like Danny. Only McIntyre is an artist, so he has an excuse for looking like a tramp.

'I'm working on a new collection,' McIntyre enthuses, taking up his brush with a deft flick of the wrist. 'It's simply called La Derriere and Samantha here is helping me realize my dream.'

The pair cast their eyes over his painting. A perfectly

rounded posterior is taking shape on the canvas. The lines are slightly exaggerated, the waist narrow, accentuating the curves and cleft.

McIntyre turns to Danny. 'Are you interested in bottoms?'

The plump copper's face turns a delightful shade of red. 'Er...not my cup of tea, really,' he stutters awkwardly.

The scruffy artist then addresses Claire. She feels his eyes roam over her body.

'Pity,' he says, 'because, if you don't mind me saying, your wife has a fine rump.'

Surprisingly she doesn't feel any discomfort at the unmasked sexual attention she is receiving but she's not sure how Danny will react, whether he'll play his part and defend her honour. If truth were told she feels rather flattered. No one ever really pays much attention to her butt and she's rather proud of it.

'Coming from an artist, I'll take that as a compliment,' Danny replies.

Marcus lets out a deep belly laugh before returning his attention to the painting.

'We're interested in buying some of your work,' Claire says.

'Music to my ears,' Marcus muses. 'But unfortunately I'm rather short of offerings. You see, we had a bit of trouble.'

'Oh, dear,' Claire sympathizes.

'But fear not, I'm having a private viewing tonight at eight and you're both very welcome to come. It'll be an intimate little affair. Do say you'll come.'

'We'd be delighted,' Claire smiles.

As they turn to leave the studio, McIntyre winks at her.

'Perhaps you'll let me add your bottom to my

collection,' he whispers, just out of earshot of Danny.

'Dirty old perv!' Danny mutters as they make the journey back to the lodge that evening, dressed to the nines for the private viewing. Claire is wearing a figure hugging off-the-shoulder black dress while Danny has selected a rather sober dark suit.

'He's an artist,' Claire snaps. 'What do you expect?'

'He took a shine to you.'

Claire shakes her head; long brunette locks brush across her bare shoulders. 'I'm not even going to dignify that with an answer.'

But deep down she is looking forward to the party. She found the artwork deeply arousing and is intrigued by the man behind the paintings. Of course it's simply professional curiosity. Or so she tells herself as they speed along the empty country lane.

There are a couple of luxury motors in the courtyard when they arrive. They park up beside an Aston Martin and step casually into the gallery area of the studio. McIntyre greets them immediately.

Inside, half a dozen smartly dressed people mill around the open plan room, champagne glasses in hand. McIntyre looks out of place – he's still in his scruffy paint-stained overalls and there's a brush tucked behind his ear. Danny makes a beeline for the bar while McIntyre takes Claire's arm and introduces her to his various other guests. There are a couple of rich art collectors, a merchant banker and the owner of a local gallery. All will be useful contacts in Claire's investigation, and for now all are potential suspects. The only person she recognizes is Samantha who is gliding around the room, serving drinks from a silver tray and entertaining the gathering with small talk.

'They're all a bit stuffy, I'm afraid,' McIntyre whispers as he steers Claire away from his other guests. 'They don't really appreciate my work. They just see me as an investment, a means of swelling their bulging bank accounts. You, on the other hand, appear to understand exactly what I'm trying to say.'

Over the course of the evening Claire and Danny work the room, chatting with the guests, subtly finding out how much they know, hoping one glass of champagne too many will cause one of them to let a vital clue slip. And as she mentally collates the snippets of conversation, Claire finds the finger of suspicion pointing in one direction – McIntyre. But she needs more than gossip before she can be sure. The brand new Range Rover suggests he's made a big sale recently, but with his paintings stolen and no new work available, she wonders how he could afford such an extravagance. Everything points to an insurance job.

They study the artwork adorning the walls, all of the pieces sumptuously erotic depictions of the female form, explicit visual feasts of flesh focussing on buxom bottoms and beautiful breasts.

Never before has Claire studied the female body in such detail. There's no doubting McIntyre's skill for capturing the unadulterated sensuality of woman, the corruptible curves and the secretive shadows where the imagination is left to roam unchecked, to fill in the blanks denied the eye by the artist's teasing reluctance to reveal all. It is sheer sexual extravagance, highly provocative yet frustratingly restrained.

Claire fantasizes about being able to afford one of McIntyre's paintings. There is one that captures her imagination completely – a wonderfully simple nude caught from behind, taut round arse cheeks tapering into a

206

delightfully narrow waist. The breasts are perfectly pert, eyes gazing longingly back over a porcelain white shoulder, seizing her gaze and drawing her in. Claire imagines the picture hanging on the wall at the end of her bed, the attractive young woman coveting her as she sleeps. She imagines admiring the image, wallowing in its sensuality as she touches herself.

'Looks can be deceptive.'

McIntyre snaps Claire out of her daydream. He's standing behind her, admiring his work. The tingling in her pussy slowly subsides.

She nods. 'You've truly captured her beauty.'

'I wasn't talking about the picture,' he whispers.

She turns, confusion furrowing her brow.

'I meant what I said earlier…about drawing you,' McIntyre adds.

'Like that?'

'My other guests are taking full advantage of my copious hospitality and your husband seems quite captivated by young Samantha. I don't think they would miss us for a couple of hours.'

'I couldn't,' Claire says.

'You have the perfect figure,' McIntyre assures her. 'It seems such a pity not to share it with the world.'

Claire casts her gaze back at the painting. The thought of being portrayed in such a strikingly erotic manner fills her with a sudden vigour. Perhaps she's had too much champagne.

'Okay then,' she nods.

McIntyre leads her from the gallery into his studio.

'How do you want me?' Claire asks.

'Naked,' he replies.

As McIntyre prepares his easel, Claire unzips her dress

and lets it slip to the floor, revealing a black full-length slip. She pulls this off over her head without a second thought and eases her panties down her thighs. She steps up onto the box occupied earlier in the day by Samantha.

'I heard you had some paintings stolen,' Claire prompts, convinced now that he knows more than he has let on.

McIntyre nods solemnly without looking up. 'It's a terrible business.'

'Have the police any idea who took them?'

'Not a clue.'

'And have you?'

McIntyre looks up from his easel and Claire notes he is momentarily speechless as he surveys her naked body.

'They'll be in a private collection by now. I doubt I'll ever see them again.'

Remembering the painting on the gallery wall, Claire adopts a similar stance, studying McIntyre as he sharpens his pencil with a penknife, long smooth strokes whittling the lead into a sharp point.

'I'm ready when you are,' she says.

He steps across to her, studying every inch of her body.

'I thought I'd do a few rough sketches first. Do you mind…?' he asks.

She shakes her head and his warm hands alight on her body, easing her around until he is completely happy with her pose.

The artist returns to his easel and begins to draw, effortless strokes gliding across the virgin paper as his eyes flit between her and the work in progress. Claire wonders how he will portray her, whether he will manipulate the lines in her favour.

She's comfortable with her body. At times she wishes

her breasts were bigger and her buttocks smaller. But doesn't every woman?

'Let's try something else,' he suggests, pinning up another sheet of paper. 'Perhaps you could hold your buttocks, pull them apart slightly.'

She does as he asks. 'Like this?'

'Yes,' he replies excitedly, 'Bend forward a little…and a little more. Oh, yes, nice taut flesh, and what a delightfully tight little anus.'

The words excite Claire as she points her arse up so he can get a better view, her fingers clawing into the skin, aware his eyes are roaming across her exposed butt and the hairy mound of her pussy. She's leaning right over now, can see McIntyre through her legs. His pencil is darting across the paper. And she can see it is not just his hand that is active. There's a growing bulge in his trousers. He is clearly enjoying his work.

'Pull those cheeks apart some more,' McIntyre enthuses, 'Oh, yes, what an exquisite arse hole you possess! The delicate tones of the smooth skin on your perfectly rounded cheeks are a joy to behold. Sheer joy!'

Claire finds his enthusiasm infectious, his voice hypnotic, and she all but forgets the investigation. She is enjoying herself – and the attention – too much.

'Do you like having your bum played with?' McIntyre asks.

From Claire's point of view, it is something that happens all too rarely. There's too much work and too little play in her life.

'I love it,' she says.

McIntyre steps away from his easel. In a second he's standing behind her, his cupped hands clasping her firm buttocks, his thumbs probing determinedly into the dark cleft between her cheeks.

'I worship women's bottoms,' he sighs. 'Everything about them is so beautiful. And yours is one of the most beautiful I have ever seen.'

His palms are roaming across the fleshy cheeks, moulding the supple skin. She smarts as he gently smacks her. Suddenly, by contrast there's a deliciously delicate tickling around her butt hole. She realizes McIntyre's paint brush is drifting through the valley between her cheeks, the fine horsehair teasing the ultra-sensitive skin. She fights to stop herself crying out. The sensation is tantalizingly subtle yet so incredibly powerful. She can't resist. It's absolutely divine. Claire closes her eyes and exhales sharply, her legs buckling beneath her.

McIntyre's hands are back on her buttocks as she slumps down onto her knees, his thumbs pushing into the crack until the tips press against Claire's anus. She doesn't resist his advances, just pushes back onto his hands, enjoys the delightfully dirtiness of his thumbs caressing the dark wrinkled skin hidden so deep away.

He eases a thumb into her, prizes open the tight vortex, and pushes the digit up her constrictive passage. Claire's body jerks as the knobbly joint of his fat thumb stretches her.

'I'd like to lick it,' he smiles. 'Can I lick it?'

He's almost begging. She'd forgotten the power a woman can have over a man. She spots an opportunity. At first she felt exposed and vulnerable on the platform. Now she's in control. She knows he'll do anything to worship her derriere.

'Only if you do it properly,' she groans through gritted teeth.

McIntyre's lips alight on her left cheek. He licks and

210

kisses her buttock, his mouth wandering ever closer to the thumb wedged up her arse. The tip of his tongue circles her open, inviting anus until at last he slip his thumb slowly out and shoves his tongue deep into her bottom, the snaking muscle pushing even deeper into the tight black tunnel, his relentless licking causing Claire's body to shudder uncontrollably.

'Do you want to fuck my arse?' she asks, overwhelmed by desire.

'Nothing would give me greater pleasure,' he mumbles, his mouth still wedged in her crack.

'Lie down, then,' she orders, retrieving a condom from her handbag.

McIntyre is on his back on the platform in a second. Claire squats over him, the bulge in his trousers obvious below his rotund belly. She slips the zip down and eases the trousers down over McIntyre's trembling thighs. His pants follow. A beautifully solid, perfectly formed cock pops up. Rolling the condom on, she knows now how she will solve this case.

Claire swivels round, lowers her spread buttocks towards the swelling tip of the erection. She pauses, just as their skin is about to make contact. McIntyre thrusts his hips up impatiently, tries to skewer her on his pole, but she rises, thwarting his clumsy attempt at entry.

'First tell me about the stolen paintings,' Claire orders.

'What?' He is confused by the sudden impediment to progress.

'I want to know what happened to them.'

She lowers her bottom slightly, wiggling against his throbbing muscle, teasing it, ensuring McIntyre is in no doubt what the reward for information will be. It's a gamble, but she knows if he has the answer he'll soon share it.

'They were stolen.'

'Are you sure about that?'

His body writhes in barely concealed frustration beneath her.

'Maybe stolen is not entirely correct,' he admits at last.

'Go on,' she prompts, her cheeks slowly enveloping the head of his shaft, the cold stickiness of his semen smearing across her pale skin. She holds his thighs firmly to prevent him regaining control.

'I couldn't face the thought of my paintings disappearing into private collections, never to be seen by an appreciative audience,' he stammers, desperate to impale her.

She inches her buttocks down. 'So you stole your own work?'

'I simply made it disappear, for now.'

'Where is it?'

'I have a lock-up, a few miles from here…'

Smiling with satisfaction, Claire plunges down onto McIntyre, his erection driving straight up into her arse. She cries out as he stretches her dark hole wide, rubs a finger back and forth over her clit as she bounces up and down on him. She comes quickly, satisfied with a job well done.

More great books from X̄cite...

Naughty Spanking One
Twenty bottom-tingling stories to make your buttocks blush!
9781906125837 £7.99

The True Confessions of a London Spank Daddy
Memoir by Peter Jones
9781906373320 £7.99

Girl Fun One
Lesbian anthology edited by Miranda Forbes
9781906373672 £7.99

The Education of Victoria
Adventures in a Victorian finishing school
9781906373696 £7.99

Ultimate Curves
Erotic short stories edited by Miranda Forbes
9781906373788 Aug 09   £7.99

Naughty! The Xcite Guide to Sexy Fun
How To book exploring edgy, kinky sex
9781906373863 Oct 09   £9.99

For more information and great offers
please visit
www.xcitebooks.com

Ultimate Curves

New! Ultimate Curves celebrates gorgeous, sexy, curvy women. Free sign-up and registration.

www.ultimatecurves.com